WELCOME TO
LABYRINTH, TEXAS

They started down the stairs. Halfway down they could see the table of brothers, and the brothers could see them. None of them moved, however. They simply watched as the two men came down the rest of the way.

When Hammer and Van Halen reached the floor, they started for the door. Hammer was to Van Halen's right, and about two steps ahead. Just when Hammer thought they would make it to the door, he heard the sound of chairs scraping the floor.

"Now!" he said, and both he and Van Halen turned, drawing their guns.

The five brothers were all pushing their chairs back and reaching for their guns. Everyone else in the saloon ducked for cover. Seven guns fired. The brothers were woefully slow and clumsy, and probably too stupid to realize that they were throwing their lives away. . . .

* * *

This title also includes an exciting excerpt from *Journal of the Gun Years* by Richard Matheson. Ride the Wild West with Clay Halser, the fastest gun west of the Mississippi!

Also in THE GUNSMITH series

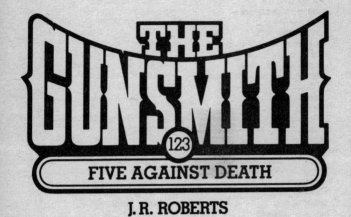

THE GUNSMITH

123

FIVE AGAINST DEATH

J. R. ROBERTS

JOVE BOOKS, NEW YORK

FIVE AGAINST DEATH

A Jove Book / published by arrangement with
the author

PRINTING HISTORY
Jove edition / March 1992

ISBN: 0-515-10810-3

Jove Books are published by The Berkley Publishing Group,
200 Madison Avenue, New York, New York 10016.
The name "JOVE" and the "J" logo
are trademarks belonging to Jove Publications, Inc.

PRINTED IN THE UNITED STATES OF AMERICA

10 9 8 7 6 5 4 3 2 1

PROLOGUE
Barlow, Oklahoma

I

Fred Hammer took one last puff on his cigar, then dropped it to the boardwalk and stubbed it out with the toe of his boot. He made sure that his gun slid loosely in his holster, then brushed aside the batwing doors of the Ace Deuce Saloon and entered.

Since Hammer was a black man who stood a little over six feet four, he immediately attracted attention as he entered. All eyes followed him as he walked to the bar and ordered a beer. The bartender stared at the big black man, dressed in black, for a few moments, and then drew the beer. Afterward, he would dispose of the mug.

"Thank you," Hammer said. He drank half the beer and set the mug down on the bar. "I'm looking for a man named Clay Van Halen. Do you know him?"

"Sure, I know him," the bartender said. "Everybody knows him."

"Where is he?"

"He's upstairs, with Karen."

"Which room?"

"Four," the man said. "All the door have numbers. Karen's is room four."

Hammer picked up the beer, finished it, dropped a coin on the bartop, and said, "Thanks."

He turned, and his eyes fell on a table near the back wall. There were five men sitting at it, and they all looked enough alike to be brothers—which was to say, they were all big and ugly.

Hammer walked to the stairway, aware that everyone's eyes were still on him. The men wondered about him. The women wondered, too, but for a different reason.

In the upstairs hallway he located room four and knocked on the door. As soon as he knocked he stepped to the side. There was a shot, and a hole appeared in the door. It was identical to the other three holes that were already there.

"Van Halen?"

"Go away."

"It's Fred Hammer, Van," Hammer said.

There was a pause and then Van Halen's voice said, "Hammer? Is that you?"

"Yeah, it's me," Hammer said. "I'm comin' in so you can tell me what the hell is goin' on."

"All right," Van Halen said, "come ahead."

Hammer shook his head, turned the doorknob, and entered the room. Van Halen was on the bed with a buxom strawberry blonde who was naked and not shy about it. Her big breasts had pink nipples and heavy, rounded undersides. She had a thick-lipped, almost sloppy-looking mouth that was oddly erotic. Immediately, Fred Hammer wondered how that mouth would feel on his body.

"Hey, Hammer," Van Halen said. He got up off the bed, naked except for the gun he held in his hand.

He was as tall as Hammer, but so painfully thin that you could see every one of his ribs. Hammer looked at the thing swinging between his legs and shook his head.

"What the hell's goin' on, Van?"

"Well," Van Halen said, scratching his unruly, sand-colored hair, "believe it or not, I came here two days ago to meet you, and I got into trouble."

"Believe it or not?" Hammer repeated. "Why would I have trouble believing that, Van? Jesus, can't you stay out of trouble for a minute?"

"It's not my fault," Van said. "Jesus, I bumped into a guy at the bar and spilled some beer on him, and he goes for his gun. What was I supposed to do?"

"You killed him."

Van turned to the girl on the bed and said, "Did I have a choice?"

The girl, Karen, was looking at Hammer and didn't hear the question.

"No," Van said, answering his own question, "no, I didn't."

Karen, her eyes still on Hammer—like she was a cat and he was a saucer of milk—licked her ample lips and put both hands beneath her breasts to heft them. Holding them like that, she touched her thumbs to her nipples.

"So what's the problem?"

"The guy had brothers," Van said, "lots of brothers."

"The five men sitting downstairs?"

"They're still there, huh?" Van said. "I been holed up here for almost two days."

"Shooting through the door?"

"I ain't givin' nobody a chance to come in here and get me," Van said. "I figured to just wait here until you got here, and then we could walk out together."

On the bed Karen had abandoned her breasts and now had both hands buried in her crotch. Her head was rolling back, and her tongue was playing around her lips, wetting them. For the first time Van noticed what she was doing.

"Hey, Hammer," he said, "Karen likes you."

Hammer stared at Karen, painfully aware of the pulsing erection he had. She knew it, too, because she was looking right at his crotch.

"Van," Hammer said, "we have to leave. We have to meet some people."

"Who we meetin'?"

"Dan Horne and Carlotta Cortez."

"Carlotta Cortez?" Van said. "Do I know her?" He knew Horne by reputation.

"No," Hammer said. "She's recruitin' Horne, and we'll meet them in Texas. From there we'll head down to Mexico for the job."

"You sure you don't want to try some of this first?" Van asked, indicating Karen. The girl was on the verge of having her eyes roll up into her head, and suddenly Hammer's erection deflated.

"She looks like she's doin' fine without me," Hammer said. "Come on, we got to go. Get dressed."

Van looked at the woman on the bed and then reached for his clothes.

"Come to think of it," he said to Hammer, "she never did seem satisfied with me. I guess I don't make her feel as good as she makes herself feel."

II

When Van Halen was dressed, he and Hammer left the room and started down the hall.

"I counted five downstairs," Hammer said. "Are there any more?"

"No," Van Halen said. "Five should be it."

"They any good?"

"Shit, how do I know?" Van Halen said. "I only met one of them, and only briefly."

"Yeah," Hammer said, "just long enough to kill him."

They came to the steps and looked down.

"How do you want to play it?" Van Halen asked.

"Straight on," Hammer said. "We'll start for the door and take it from there."

"Okay."

"If anything happens," Hammer said, "I'll take center and right of center. You take left."

"That gives you three and me two."

"You want to argue the point?"

"No."

"Let's go."

They started down the stairs. Halfway down they could see the table of brothers, and the brothers could see them. None of them moved, however. They simply watched as the two men came down the rest of the way.

When Hammer and Van Halen reached the floor, they started for the door. Hammer was to Van Halen's right, and about two steps ahead. That was so if they had to turn, they wouldn't be in each other's way.

Just when Hammer thought they would make it to the door, he heard the sound of chairs scraping the floor.

"Now!" he said, and both he and Van Halen turned, drawing their guns.

The five brothers were all pushing their chairs back and reaching for their guns. Everyone else in the saloon ducked for cover. Seven guns fired.

Hammer fired at the brother in the center, then turned his attention to the two on the right. They were woefully slow and clumsy, and probably too stupid to realize that they were throwing their lives away.

Van Halen fired at the two men on the left, killing them easily.

When it was over, the brothers littered the floor, and the others in the saloon were staring at Hammer and Van Halen.

Hammer ejected the spent shells from his gun and reloaded before holstering it. Van Halen followed his example.

"Time to go," Hammer said. "Where's your horse?"

"It was out front," Van Halen said, "but that was two days ago."

"There are a bunch of horses out front," Hammer said. "Must belong to them. If yours isn't there, you can take one of theirs."

"Right."

"Hey," the bartender yelled, "you can't leave! You got to wait for the sheriff!"

"Let him catch up to us," Hammer said, "if he really wants to."

ONE

Clint Adams stepped from his hotel in Labyrinth, Texas, and took a deep breath. He'd been back here from Sacramento, California, testing himself. He wanted to see how long he could stay in Labyrinth before something he couldn't understand drove him to leave. The unnamed thing that existed inside men who traveled—not that they had anyplace to go, they simply felt they had to have a horse beneath them, or a rig, or a train.

Clint had been back a month. He didn't think he had ever spent a whole month in town. Now that he had, he was starting to feel closed in.

He walked down the street to a small café that opened early to serve breakfast. He had eggs, bacon, spuds, biscuits, and a pot of coffee. Although there was no shortage of women in town who would want to share his bed—primarily the women who worked for his friend Rick Hartman in his saloon—Clint had spent last night alone. That was part and parcel of the closed-in feeling he was suffering. So was eating breakfast alone. Most of the time he went to the saloon and had breakfast with his friend Rick. For the past three mornings he had eaten breakfast alone at this café.

7

"Another pot of coffee?" Andy Anderson asked. He was the fiftyish, bookish-looking man who owned the café. He did the cooking and the serving.

"I don't think so, Andy," Clint said. "One's enough today."

"You feelin' all right?" Andy asked.

"Just out of sorts, a bit," Clint said. He stood up and handed the man some money.

"This is too much—" Andy started to protest.

"Keep it," Clint said. "You've got the best breakfast in town."

"Don't tell that to T. C.," Andy said. T. C. was the black bartender at Rick's saloon and also was an excellent cook.

"I won't."

Clint left the café and started walking. At one point he stopped and bought a copy of the local newspaper. He folded it up and carried it in his left hand. Habits of a lifetime died hard, as he kept his right hand—his gun hand—free.

He took his time this morning, walking around town, and finally found himself standing in front of Rick's Place, his friend Rick Hartman's saloon. He knocked on the door, which was opened by T. C.

"If you're here for breakfast," the muscular black man said, "you're late."

"How about coffee?"

T. C. pretended to consider the question, then said, "That can be arranged," and let Clint in.

"Well," Rick said from his table, "what brings you here?"

"I brought you your newspaper," Clint said, holding it up.

"Thanks," Rick said. "Pull up a chair."

Clint sat, and T. C. brought him a coffee cup. There was already a pot of coffee on the table. He picked it up and poured.

"So?" Rick asked. "What's on your mind?"

"What makes you ask that?"

"Come on," Rick said. "You haven't been here for breakfast in three days. You haven't played poker in five. You just sit in the corner and nurse beers. Last night you broke my girls' hearts by going home alone. When are you going to admit it to yourself?"

"Admit what?" Clint asked, sipping his coffee.

"You're ready to hit the trail again," Rick said.

"To where?"

"To anywhere."

Clint sipped his coffee.

"Hey," Rick said, "I think a month is pretty good, but who needs you around here if you're going to sulk?"

Clint stared at his friend and said, "Don't hold back, Rick. Give it to me straight."

Rick smiled and leaned forward.

"Leave, Clint," he said, "tomorrow. For your own good—and mine."

Clint regarded his friend across the table for a few moments. Rick Hartman was an excellent business-man, and he had friends and contacts all over the country. His ultimate goal was to have a gambling palace in San Francisco. Clint felt that beyond that, his friend would be very successful if he decided to go into politics.

"I don't know how you do it," Clint said.

"Do what?"

"Stay in one place for so long."

Rick smiled and said, "It's called being normal. A

lot of people have the same problem. It's one you'll never have, my friend."

"What? Being normal, or staying in one place for a long time?"

"Either," Rick said, "both. It's time for you to move on, my friend. Get it out of your system, and then come back."

Clint smiled at his friend and said, "All right, but I've got to have a direction in mind."

"North," Rick said.

"South," T. C. said.

"East or west," Clint said. "Tough decision."

"Maybe something will happen to help you make up your mind," Rick said.

"Well, it better happen fast," Clint said. "I'm taking your advice and leaving tomorrow."

TWO

Clint felt better, having made the decision to leave in the morning. He spent the rest of the day getting his rig and team together and making sure that Duke, his big black gelding, was ready to go.

Later that evening he went to Rick's to have a steak with his friend on his last night in town. As usual, Rick's Place was packed with drinkers and gamblers, each getting their fill.

Clint was eating his steak and talking with Rick, who had his current lady, a blonde named Monica, sitting next to him. When a lull fell over the place, Clint and Rick looked up to see what had caused it.

"Jesus," Monica said.

A big black man, dressed all in black and smoking a cigar, was standing just inside the batwing doors. His black pants had silver along the legs, and his holster was also studded with silver.

"Who the hell is that?" Rick said.

"Hammer," Clint said.

Fred Hammer's eyes scanned the room until they finally fell on Clint Adams. The black face was creased by a wide, white smile, and he started across the room. Clint was standing by the time

11

Hammer reached him, and the two clasped hands warmly.

"What the hell are you doing here?" Clint asked, pumping his friend's hand.

"Looking for you, of course."

Clint took a moment to introduce Hammer to Rick and Monica.

"Charmed," Hammer said to Monica, kissing her hand. The blonde couldn't take her eyes off of him.

Hammer turned to Rick and extended his hand.

"I've heard a lot about you," he said.

"And I you," Rick said. "Would you like a beer?"

"I'd love one."

"Monica, honey," Rick said, "would you get Mr. Hammer a beer?"

"Just Hammer," the black man said, "no Mister."

"Certainly," Monica said, standing up, "whatever he wants."

Monica was tall and high-breasted, and she kept her back perfectly straight and thrust her chest out as she walked to the bar.

"What brings you here?" Clint asked.

"Pull up a chair, please," Rick said.

"Thanks," Hammer said, sitting. He looked at Clint and said, "I have a business proposition for you."

"Oh? What kind?"

"The kind you don't like."

Clint frowned.

"I know you don't hire your gun out," Hammer said, "so I want to borrow it."

Monica returned with Hammer's beer, which she set down in front of him, bumping his arm with her hip at the same time.

"Thank you," he said, smiling up at her.

"You're welcome."

She started to sit, but Rick stopped her.

"You and I are leaving," he said, standing up. "Clint and Hammer have a lot of catching up to do."

Reluctantly, the tall blonde allowed herself to be led away.

"Now tell me again what it is you want," Clint said. "I don't think I heard you right the first time."

"I need to borrow your gun."

"My gun?"

"Come on, Clint," Hammer said. "I have a job and I want you to come with me."

"Where?"

"To Mexico."

"To do what?"

"To save an entire town of women and children from a bandit called *El Gigante*."

"El Gigante?"

"Yes," Fred Hammer said. "It means 'The Giant.' "

THREE

"I know what it means," Clint said. "Why do they call him that?"

Hammer shrugged, puffing on his thin cigar.

"I guess we'll find out when we get there."

"Oh, no," Clint said. "*You'll* find out when *you* get there."

"Oh, come on," Hammer said, his tone cajoling. "Didn't you hear what I said? There's a whole town of women and children who need help."

"How did you find out about this?"

"Carlotta Cortez."

"Who is Carlotta Cortez?"

"She's a very impressive lady, Clint, and she lives in Los Alamos, a small town well south of the border. This town is populated by women and children, mostly. The men who are there are elderly. Carlotta Cortez came north looking for help in fighting off the bandit *El Gigante*."

"What makes you think this bandit hasn't already taken over the town?"

"He's demanded tribute from the people of the town, and he gave them a month to collect it. There are two weeks left, and it'll take us a week of hard

14

riding to get there. That'll give us a week to size
things up and devise a defense."

"Tell me," Clint said, "how many men do you have
for this little job?"

"Well . . ." Hammer said, "I've got three . . . so
far . . . and Carlotta Cortez."

"How many more men do you figure you'll add to
your little army?"

"Uh . . . well, when you sign on, that'll be . . . uh,
it."

"Five?" Clint said. "Five people against *El Gigante*
and his *bandidos*?"

Hammer twirled his cigar in his mouth with his
left hand, staring at Clint over the burning tip.

"To tell you the truth," he said, "I wasn't able to get
as many men as I wanted, but then, the money isn't
real good. Los Alamos isn't exactly a wealthy town.
What money they make comes from whatever they
can make with their own hands, and then sell."

"I see," Clint said. "Exactly how much are you paying the men you have?"

"A hundred dollars each."

"A hundred dollars?" Clint asked. "To risk their
lives?"

"Well," Hammer said, "a hundred dollars and
found. If and when we, uh, defeat *El Gigante,* who
knows what kinds of treasures he has?"

"Oh, now I get it," Clint said. "You're on a treasure hunt." It was all falling into place now. Clint
leaned forward and said, "Wait a minute! You're paying them a hundred dollars out of your own pocket,
aren't you?"

Hammer took the cigar out of his mouth and stared
down at it.

"I'll cut you in for half, Clint," he said. "Half whatever we recover from the *bandidos*."

"Hammer—"

"At least meet my partners," Hammer said quickly. "Meet Carlotta. Listen to her story. Her people really need help."

"Uh-huh, and that's the real reason you're going down there," Clint said. "To help some people who are in need."

"You know why I'm going down there," Hammer said. "But if we can help them at the same time, why not?"

"Hammer—" Clint said again.

"Come on," Hammer said, "meet my . . . partners."

"Partners," Clint said dubiously.

"Well . . . colleagues, then," Hammer said.

"Just who are your colleagues?"

"There's the beautiful Carlotta, of course," Hammer said. "Quite a woman. She wears a gun and says she knows how to use it."

"Who else?"

"Dan Horne."

"I've heard of Horne," Clint said. "Good with a gun, bad with people."

"The same goes for Van Halen."

"Clay Van Halen?"

"You've heard of him, too?"

"I sure have. Brings trouble with him wherever he goes."

"That he does."

"Fair gunhands, troublemakers," Clint said, "but not top guns."

"Ah, they're better than you think," Hammer said, "but I didn't exactly have the kind of money it would have taken to hire some top guns, like Ron Diamond or . . . or yourself."

"So you decided to ask for a favor."

"There's money in it, Clint," Hammer said. "It'll just take some time to get to it."

"And some planning."

"And some planning," Hammer said, nodding. "Whataya say? Meet the others?"

Clint hesitated.

"What else have you got to do?"

That was the key question. He had nothing else to do, and he'd been looking for a direction to take.

"All right."

"You'll come?"

"I'll meet the others," Clint said, "and then make my decision."

FOUR

Across the street, in the dining room of Labyrinth's second hotel, Van Halen, Horne, and Carlotta Cortez were eating dinner.

"What's takin' him so long?" Van Halen said.

"It would take time to talk a man like the Gunsmith into something like this, no?" Carlotta Cortez asked.

"You think this Gunsmith is really somethin', don't you," Van Halen said.

"He is an *Americano* legend, is he not?"

"Legend," Van Halen said in disgust. "What do you think, Horne?"

Horne was younger than Van Halen by ten years. He had an even younger face. That and his slight size combined to cause men to underestimate him. In spite of the fact that he was barely five feet six, he was well formed and strong, and had often whipped men twice his size.

"I'll wait until I meet the man before I form an opinion."

"Ah!" Van Halen said. He looked at Carlotta, with whom he had become smitten as soon as he saw her. "You're impressed by his reputation."

"*Sí*, of course."

"Well, I got somethin' that'll impress you," Van Halen said. "Why don't we share a room tonight."

Carlotta didn't answer, but gave the man an amused look.

"Come on, *señorita,*" Van Halen said, "it'll be cheaper if we share a room."

"I will pay the extra, *señor,*" Carlotta said.

"Whatsa matter?" Van Halen demanded. "You don't like me?"

"Would that be so hard to believe, Van Halen?" Horne asked. "That there's a woman somewhere who doesn't like you?"

"Mind your business, shorty."

Horne smiled at Van Halen.

"You'd have to call me something a lot worse than that to get my goat, Van Halen," Horne said. "I've been hearing that one all my life."

"How about this one, then—" Van Halen said, but before he could finish, Carlotta cut him off.

"Silencio!" she said. "Here they come."

Van Halen turned, and Horne looked up at the doorway to the lobby.

"So that's the Gunsmith, huh?" Van Halen said. "He don't look like much."

Clint and Hammer left Rick's Place and walked across the street to Labyrinth's second hotel.

"They should be in the dining room," Hammer said as they walked through the lobby.

When they reached the doorway to the dining room, Hammer said, "There they are. Come on."

Clint didn't move. He was rooted to the spot by the sight of Carlotta Cortez.

She had a mass of black hair that cascaded

around her head and down to her shoulders. Her
eyes were almost almond-shaped, her mouth wide,
her cheekbones high. Her skin was dark, appearing
even more so by the white shirt she was wearing.
She was seated, but he could still tell that she was
full-breasted and tall.

"Clint?"

"Huh?"

"If you come into the dining room," Hammer said
into his ear, "I can introduce you to her."

"Oh," Clint said, feeling foolish.

"Come on," Hammer said, taking Clint by the
elbow, "and close your mouth."

FIVE

"This is my friend Clint Adams," Hammer said to the people at the table. "That's Clay Van Halen."

Clint nodded, but Van Halen simply gave him an arrogant stare.

"This is Dan Horne."

"Good to meet you," Horne said, extending his hand. Clint shook it briefly.

"And over there," Hammer said, "is Carlotta Cortez."

"My pleasure," Clint said to her.

"Con mucho gusto, señor," Carlotta said. "I am pleased that you are going to help us."

"I haven't agreed to anything yet," Clint said.

"No," Carlotta said, arching her beautiful eyebrows and looking at Hammer.

"I'm still tryin' to convince him," Hammer said, pulling up a chair. Clint remained standing. Hammer looked around and said, "I need to get a steak."

"What do you need to convince you, *señor*?" Carlotta asked him.

"I'm not sure."

"Is the money not enough?" Carlotta asked him.

"Oh," Hammer said, "Clint wouldn't do this for the

money, Carlotta. He doesn't hire his gun out."

"Too good for that, huh?" Van Halen asked.

"I've just never gotten into that habit," Clint said. "I've found other ways to make a living."

"Yeah, well," Van Halen said, "I've never been able to bring myself to wear a badge, myself."

"The money sure isn't a lot," Horne said, looking at Clint.

"Then what are you in for?" Van Halen asked.

Horne looked at Van Halen and said, "Let's just say I have my own reasons."

Van Halen looked at Carlotta Cortez and frowned. Ever since he had met Horne and Carlotta he'd been wondering what Carlotta had given Horne to recruit him. It bothered him that the shorter, younger Horne might have bedded the Mexican woman, as he had so far been unable to.

"And why would you take a hand, if not for the money?" Van Halen asked.

"Like Mr. Horne," Clint said, "I'd have my own reasons for buying in. What are your reasons?"

"Money is money," Van Halen said, "and when you don't have any, a little is a lot."

Clint couldn't argue with that kind if logic.

"Well," Clint said, "I have to be going."

"Why did you come over here?" Van Halen asked.

"Just to meet the rest of you before I make my decision."

Van Halen opened his mouth to comment, but Hammer silenced him with a look. Hammer then looked at Carlotta and jerked his head at her, indicating that it was her turn to try to convince Clint.

"Are you going to the saloon now?" Carlotta asked Clint.

"Yes."

"Would you mind if I came with you?" she asked, standing up. When she stood up she attracted all of the male eyes in the room. "Now that I have had dinner I think I would like a drink."

"Sure," Clint said, giving Hammer a look, "come on along."

"*Gracias.*"

She came around the table to stand next to him, but Van Halen reached out and grabbed her wrist before they could leave.

"You've got my room number, don't you, darlin'?" Van Halen said. He was trying to present the impression that they were sleeping together, for Clint's sake.

She jerked her wrist free and said, "I do not care to know your room number." She looked at Clint and said, "Shall we go?"

"See you later," Hammer said. "I'll come over for a drink after I eat."

Clint nodded, and he and Carlotta left.

After they had gone, Van Halen looked at Hammer and said, "Who does he think he is, making us wait for his decision."

"He knows who he is," Hammer said, still looking around for a waiter. "Don't ever make the mistake of asking him that to his face."

"Well . . . what about her? What makes her so high and mighty that she's too good for us?"

"I don't get the impression that she thinks she's too good for us," Hammer said, looking at Horne. "Do you?"

"No," Horne said, "I don't, either."

Van Halen frowned at both of them now, wondering if he was the only one of the three who hadn't been to bed with the Mexican woman.

Hammer stared across the table at Van Halen, wondering if the man was going to be more trouble than his gun was worth.

SIX

Clint had been the center of attention walking out of the saloon with Fred Hammer. Now he was the center of attention once again, walking in with Carlotta Cortez.

"Why don't we sit at a table?" Clint suggested.

She looked around and said, "I don't see an empty table."

"Oh," Clint said, "one will open up."

Clint looked across the room at Rick Hartman, seated at his table with Monica. Rick took the hint and said something to the blond girl. She frowned, and although she stood up when he did, it was plain that she did not like the idea.

"See?" Clint said.

He led Carlotta across the room to the table, and T. C. came over quickly to see what they wanted.

"Cerveza," she said.

"I'll have a beer, too, T. C."

"Sure," he said, a dopey smile on his face as he stared at Carlotta, "comin' up."

"You are known here?" she asked, and then rushed on without giving him a chance to reply. "But, of course, you are known everywhere."

"Well, not everywhere."

"But are you not *El*"—she started to say it in

Spanish, then stopped and said it in English—"the Gunsmith?"

"To some people, yes," Clint said.

"I do not understand."

"To people who don't know me," he explained, "I'm only the Gunsmith. To people who know me, I'm Clint Adams."

"But you are a legend, are you not?"

"I'd much rather be just a man."

T. C. came over with the beers, set them down, and stood there grinning.

"That's fine, T. C.," Clint said.

"Is there anything else I can get you?"

"No, I think this will do it."

"All right," the bartender said, "but if you do need anything else, just holler."

"We will."

As T. C. walked away, Carlotta said, "You receive excellent service."

Clint smiled and said, "I don't think I'm the reason we're receiving such good service."

She took two healthy swallows of beer and then cleaned her upper lip with her tongue. Clint thought that he could sit there buying her beer all night.

"All right," he said, "now that we're here, you can take your shot."

She frowned and tilted her head to the right, just slightly.

"My shot?"

"Take your turn at trying to convince me to come along to Mexico."

She sat straight back in her chair and studied him, looking slightly frustrated.

"I do not understand this," she said, shaking her

head. "Would you not come with us simply because your friend asked you to?"

"I don't know how it works in your country, *señorita*—" he started.

"Please," she interrupted him, "call me Carlotta."

"All right, Carlotta," Clint said. "In my country, you don't do anything just because someone asks you to, no matter how good friends you are."

"*Amigos*—friends do not help friends?"

"Yes, of course they do," Clint said, "but there are . . . different kinds of friends."

She frowned at him and said, "Now I truly do not understand. Are not friends, friends?"

"See," Clint said, trying to think of what he was trying to say, and a way to say it so she would understand, "with friends like Hammer, a favor usually involves some kind of danger."

"Well then," she said reasonably, "is that not more reason to help him, to keep him safe from danger?" She stared at him expectantly.

Clint opened his mouth to reply, then snapped it shut. She was making it very difficult for him to argue his point effectively. It was very difficult to concentrate, anyway, with her licking her upper lip like that. He noticed that while they had been talking she had worked her way very effectively through her beer. He drank his down and picked up both mugs.

"I'll get two more beers."

He walked to the bar, where Rick Hartman was standing talking to T. C.

"I told you to holler if you wanted more," T. C. said accusingly.

"I need to stretch my legs," Clint said with a shrug. "Sorry, T. C."

T. C. made a face and went to get the beers.

"What happened to Monica?" Clint asked.

"She couldn't stand the competition," Rick said. "Who is your friend? And does she want a job?"

Briefly, Clint told Rick what Fred Hammer and Carlotta Cortez wanted him to do.

"Well," Rick said, "you've been looking for a reason to leave."

"Doesn't this sound slightly dangerous to you?" Clint asked. "Going down to Mexico and taking on a band of bandits led by a man known as 'The Giant'?"

"You, of all people, are judging a man by what other people call him?"

T. C. set two beers down in front of Clint with a bang and stalked away.

"You've got a point there," Clint admitted.

"Besides," Rick said, "Hammer could be right. You could go down there, defeat this bandit and his men, and end up very rich."

"You've got a point there, too," Clint said, picking up the beers.

"Have you listened to the lady's full story yet?" Rick asked.

"No."

"Why don't you do that before you decide?"

Clint stared at his friend and said, "What makes you so smart?"

"I'm never personally involved in decisions like this," Rick said. "That can make you very smart."

Clint stared at his friend for a few moments and then said, "So that's been my problem all these years."

Rick smiled and said, "Live and learn."

SEVEN

Across the street in the hotel dining room, Fred Hammer was cutting into a rare steak, watching the blood run across the plate.

"Well," Van Halen said, "I'm gonna see if this town has a whorehouse." He stood up and looked down at Horne. "What about you, kid?"

"I think I'll have some more coffee," Horne said. "Thanks just the same."

"Suit yourself, kid."

"If you're going to keep calling me 'kid,'" Horne said, "I'd prefer you call me 'shorty.'"

Van Halen grinned and said, "Sure, kid."

As Van Halen left, Horne called the waiter over and ordered another pot of coffee.

"You got any pie?"

"Yes, sir," the man said, "apple, peach, and blueberry."

"I'll have the apple."

"Yes, sir."

"Save me a piece," Hammer said. "I'll have it after my steak."

"Of course . . . sir," the waiter said, not looking at Hammer.

"Does that ever bother you?" Horne asked.

"Does what ever bother me?" Hammer asked.

"The way they treat you . . . you know, because you're black?"

Hammer smiled, showing Horne very white teeth.

"No, it don't bother me, Horne," he said. "The way I look at it, if me bein' black bothers them, that's their problem."

"Yeah," Horne said, "that's about how I feel about being short."

Hammer frowned.

"You comparin' bein' black to bein' short?"

"Well," Horne said, "there isn't a whole lot either one of us can do to change it, is there?"

Hammer thought that over for a moment, using his tongue to free a piece of meat from between two of his teeth, and then said, "How about that."

The waiter brought the coffee and Horne's pie.

"I'm sorry . . . sir," the waiter said, "but we have no more apple pie."

"Here," Horne said to Hammer, "you can have this piece."

"Never mind," Hammer said. He looked at the waiter and said, "Do you have any peach left?"

"Uh, yes . . . sir."

"Well, my good man, I'll have a slice of the peach," Hammer said.

"Yes . . . sir."

As the waiter turned to walk away, Hammer grabbed him by the sleeve.

"Don't forget, friend," he said, "it's promised to me, right?"

The waiter swallowed hard and said, "Uh, of course . . . sir."

Hammer released him and he scurried away.

At another table three men were sitting, watching. One of them threw down his napkin and walked over to Hammer's table.

"Hey, boy," he said.

Hammer ignored him.

Horne looked up and looked at the man.

"You talkin' to me?"

"Hell, no," the man said, "I ain't talkin' to you, I'm talkin' to your nigger. Hey, boy, I'm talkin' to you."

"I'm eatin' my dinner," Hammer said, cutting into his meat. "If you want to talk to me, I suggest you wait until I'm finished."

"Wha—" the man said. He was a large man, maybe as tall as Hammer, but he outweighed the black man, most of that weight hanging over his belt.

He turned around to look at his friends and said, "We got us an uppity nigger here."

Unfortunately for the man, he was wearing a tie. Hammer reached up with his left hand, grasped the tie firmly, and yanked down. His hand went past the table, so that the man's forehead slammed into it, almost upsetting it. With his right hand Hammer pressed the tip of the steak knife against the man's chest.

"When I let you go," he said into the man's ear, "you're gonna turn around and go back to your table. If you don't, we're gonna see if this here steak knife is sharp enough to go through your heart. Now I know you understand me, don't you?"

"Mmm-hmm," the man mumbled.

"Good," Hammer said. He released his hold on the man's tie and was cutting into his meat before the man straightened up.

Horne watched the man carefully, even though he knew Hammer probably didn't need the backup. The man put his hand to his head, probably checking for blood. There was none, but there was a bump rising there. He stood there for about another three seconds, then turned and walked unsteadily back to his table, his back and neck stiff. Other diners in the room had watched the entire tableau and were now finding other things to look at.

Horne took his hand off his gun and relaxed—but just a bit.

"Let's keep an eye on that table," Hammer said without looking up. "His friends might push him to get brave, and they might back him."

"Right."

"What were we talking about?"

Horne ate a piece of apple pie, which wasn't bad, and said, "I was going to ask you what we were going to do if Adams says no."

"He won't," Hammer said, "but just for the sake of argument, we'll be leaving in the mornin', one way or another."

"What makes you think he'll come?"

"I know him," Hammer said. "He's been here too long, he's my friend . . . and he's spending some time with Carlotta."

"What's in it for him?" Horne asked.

"Satisfaction," Hammer said. "The man just has to have a cause to fight for, and right now Carlotta is givin' him one."

Hammer paused over his steak, chewing thoughtfully on the piece in his mouth and said, "Oh, yeah, he'll come, all right."

EIGHT

"Tell me about Los Alamos," Clint said when he returned to the table.

"It is a small town," she said. "Once it was an abandoned town—how do you say it here?"

"A ghost town," Clint said.

"*Sí,*" she said, nodding, "a ghost town. Little by little, people came to live, most of them women, many with children."

"Why?"

"*Perdón?*"

"Why women?"

"They had no men," she said. "They needed a place to live."

"What happened to their men?"

"They were killed by *bandidos,* or executed by the government," Carlotta said, "or they simply . . . went away."

"All right."

"As time went by, it became known that many women lived there, with very few men. Other women came, and soon the town was alive again."

"How did you get there?"

33

"I was born there," she said.

Clint frowned.

"How old are you?"

"Twenty-two."

Clint stared at her. He'd thought she was in her late twenties. It wasn't so much that she looked older, but that she carried herself with such assurance.

The young did not usually have that.

"Then, this town has existed for a long time?"

"*Si,*" she said, "I was the first child born there."

"But you said there were few men."

"My mother was with child when she found her way there," Carlotta said. "My father did not want children. He left my mother when she became pregnant."

"I see."

"We make our living with our hands," she said. "Quilts, jewelry, whatever we can make, we sell. We grow our own food. We are a poor town."

"Then what does *El Gigante* want from you?" Clint asked. "How can he expect tribute from you if you have nothing?"

She paused to sip beer and lick her upper lip. Clint shifted in his chair, trying to get comfortable with the swelling that was inside his pants.

"There is a rumor," she said, "that Los Alamos, that we have a . . . a treasure."

Clint frowned. He wondered if Hammer knew about this rumor. Maybe the black man was on more of a treasure hunt than he let on.

"It's not true?"

"No," she said, "it is not."

He didn't know her well enough to tell if she was lying or not.

"Go on."

"*El Gigante* says we must pay him tribute, or he will destroy us. We decided that we must find help, and I was sent to hire men to help us."

"And you found Hammer?"

"I was fortunate," she said. "I found him almost immediately. He said that he would gather some men and come back with me."

"He hasn't gathered very many, has he?"

"No," she said, "but he says that the ones he has are very good. He also said—"

"What did he also say?" Clint asked.

"That you and he were worth any ten men."

"How many men does *El Gigante* have?"

"We are not sure," she said, "but we believe he has at least forty."

"Forty," Clint said, "against four."

"Five," she said. "I know how to use a gun, *Señor* Adams."

"Clint," he said, "call me Clint."

"Clint."

"Tell me, Carlotta," Clint said, "how many people live in Los Alamos?"

"Fifty-three," she said. "Twenty-nine women—ten of them over sixty—seven men, and seventeen children."

"Seven men?"

"*Sí,*" she said. "The youngest is fifty-four."

"Is there anyone else from your town who knows how to use a gun besides you?"

"Very few," she said, "but they are willing to learn."

Clint thought a moment, then asked, "How old are the children?"

"The oldest is seventeen, the youngest is an infant," Carlotta said. She leaned forward, moved as if to touch his hand, then pulled back as if his hand were hot. "It is for the children that I fear the most."

"Uh-huh," he said, "yeah."

Across the street Hammer finished his pie and said, "I'm going across to the saloon to see how Carlotta is doing."

"Do you think she can convince him to come?"

"She convinced you, didn't she?" Hammer said. "Besides, if she can't convince him, no one can. You comin'?"

"No," Horne said, "I think I'll turn in."

"Be ready to move out at first light."

"I'll be ready."

Hammer took one sidelong glance at the table with the three men. The one he'd had the altercation with was still feeling the bump on his head with his hand.

"Watch yourself with them," Hammer said.

"Don't worry," Horne said.

As Hammer walked from the dining room he felt sure that young Dan Horne was watching his back. In the few days they'd known each other he had come to like Horne. He hadn't seen him in action yet, but he felt sure the younger man would pull his weight.

As for Van Halen, it was the other way around. Hammer had known Van Halen for about five years. Once he was more than a fair hand with a gun, but he seemed to have gone back some over the years.

Consequently, at the moment he had a little more confidence in Horne than he did in Van Halen.

Jesus, Hammer thought as he crossed the lobby, he really needed Clint to make this work.

NINE

Clint saw Hammer as soon as he entered, and waved. The place was so packed now that Hammer caused only a ripple in the attention span of the drinkers and gamblers.

When Clint waved, Carlotta turned to see who he was waving at. When she saw Hammer, she stood up.

"Are you leaving?" Clint asked.

"Yes," she said, "I must get some sleep. We will be leaving early."

Clint stood up.

"If you are coming with us," she said, "I will see you in the morning."

"Tell me, Carlotta," Clint said, "does your town have a saloon?"

"A *cantina*? Of course."

"Does it serve beer?"

"Yes," she said. "Why?"

"Never mind," he said. "Good night."

As she passed Hammer they exchanged a greeting. Clint watched her until she was out the door. Her passing caused much more than a ripple.

Clint was thinking it might be worth going to

Mexico just to see her lick beer off her upper lip again.

Dan Horne held his seat until the three men had gotten up from their table. He waited until they were in the lobby, then got up and followed them. From the dining room entrance he saw them leave the hotel. He walked quickly to the door to watch them cross the street to the saloon.

He decided it wasn't quite time to turn in after all.

As Carlotta left the saloon she saw three men crossing the street toward her. She had to pass them to get to the hotel. She noticed that one of them had a large lump on his forehead.

"Hey," one of them said as she approached them, "seen-yore-rita. Wanna party?"

"Not with you, *señor*," she said.

She continued walking, but one of them—the man with the lump—grabbed her arm as she went by.

"Hey, lady—" he started.

She turned quickly and, using the heel of her hand, slapped him right on the red lump on his forehead.

"Ow!" he cried, releasing her arm.

She turned and walked away quickly.

"By golly," one of the other men said, "everybody's pickin' on you tonight, Seth."

"Damn she-devil," the man called Seth complained. "I oughtta—"

"Let's go get a drink, Seth," one of his friends told him.

Reluctantly, Seth allowed himself to be pulled toward the saloon.

• • •

Horne was still standing in the doorway when Carlotta reached the hotel.

"I thought you might need help, but I guess I was wrong."

"Gracias, señor," she said, "for the thought."

"Is Hammer in the saloon?"

"Sí," she said, "with *Señor Adams.*"

"Are you going to bed now?"

"Sí, I am very tired, and we will be starting out early in the morning."

Carlotta was several inches taller than Horne, but somehow she avoided looking down at him. He liked her for that. He would have offered to walk her to her room if he thought there was a chance she would say yes. In fact, he would have done much more than that if . . .

"And you?" she asked.

"I think I'll take some air and then turn in, too," he said.

"Buenas noches, then."

"Good night."

As Carlotta entered the hotel, Horne stepped down off the boardwalk and crossed the street.

Clay Van Halen managed to find a whore with black hair. When they got to her room he undressed and was already hard. He waited for her to make a comment about what she saw.

"My," she said, "you sure are hung for a skinny man, aren't you?"

"And all of it is yours, babe," he said. "All you got to do is get on all fours."

She shucked her loose-fitting dress, showing that

she had nothing on underneath. Her breasts were small, but she was as tall as Carlotta Cortez, and when she turned around and got down on all fours on the bed she had a nice ass.

Van Halen got on the bed behind her, grabbed her by her hips, and thought about Carlotta Cortez. . . .

TEN

"I hope it wasn't something I said," Hammer commented as he sat opposite Clint.

"Have you ever watched her drink beer?" Clint asked Hammer.

Hammer smiled and said, "Ain't that somethin'?"

Clint waved at T. C., but the black bartender either didn't see him, or was pretending not to see him. One of Rick's girls, a redhead named Olga, came over and leaned on Clint's shoulder.

"Can I get you or your handsome friend anything, Clint, honey?"

"Sure can, Olga," Clint said. "We could use a couple of beers. I don't think T. C. is talking to me these days."

"Comin' right up, hon."

She ran her forefinger along Hammer's jaw and went to get the beers.

"Friend of yours?"

"Friend of everybody," Clint said.

"So what did you think of Carlotta?" Hammer asked.

"Very impressive."

"She is that."

"Is her story on the level?"

"All that stuff about women and children—what was it, seventeen children?"

"That's what she said."

"I guess we won't know for sure if it's on the level until we get there. Uh, are you coming?"

Olga came over with the beers, pressed her warm hip against Hammer's shoulder, and put them down on the table.

"Anythin' else?"

"If there is," Hammer said, "I'll be sure to call you, babe."

"I'll be waitin', honey."

She turned and hip-twitched her way across the room.

"You know," Clint said, "I think I'll come along with you to Mexico."

"Well, good," Hammer said. "That's a load off my mind. Horne and Van Halen are okay, but with you along I know we've got a shot at this."

They each took a long pull on their beers. Clint spotted three men standing at the bar, watching them. One of them had a nasty-looking lump on his head.

"Friends of yours?" Clint asked.

Hammer eased around to take a look, then faced Clint.

"I put that lump on his head."

"Why?"

"He interrupted my dinner."

"Think they followed you here?"

"Naw," Hammer said, "they're probably just lookin' for an after-dinner drink."

"I hope you're right."

"So tell me," Hammer said, "how did our Carlotta convince you to come along?"

"She said a few things," Clint said, "but one thing in particular stood out."

"I wonder what that was."

"She said that when a friend is facing danger, you're supposed to go along and protect him from it."

"She said that?"

"Yep."

"And that's the reason you're comin' along?" Hammer said. "Clint, I'm touched."

"Also," Clint said, "I want to see her lick beer from her upper lip again."

Hammer raised his beer mug and said, "Amen, brother."

Seth Williams stood at the bar, downing beers and staring at Fred Hammer through the mirror behind the bar.

"Forget it, Seth," his friend Hal Morris told him. "The black is sittin' with Clint Adams."

"You don't want any part of Adams," his other friend, Tully Blake, said.

"I know I don't want Adams," Seth Williams said, "but I want that uppity black bastard. Are you fellas with me, or not?"

Morris and Blake exchanged a glance and then Morris said, "We're with you, Seth, as long as it don't include taking on the Gunsmith."

"All right, then," Williams said. "Let's wait outside for that smart black bastard. He's got to leave here sometime."

Williams pushed away from the bar and stalked toward the door, and his two friends followed.

• • •

"Your friends are leaving," Clint said.

"I ain't worried."

"Just watch your step when you leave."

Hammer waved his hand, further indicating that he wasn't worried.

"What time does this place close?"

"Late," Clint said, "very late."

"What about the girls?" he asked. "They work after closing?"

"You'll have to ask them."

"I was thinking about that redheaded girl, Olga."

Clint stood up and dropped some money on the table.

"I'm turning in, Hammer," Clint said. "I'll be in front of your hotel at first light."

"You still riding that big black monster?"

"Duke," Clint said. "You bet."

"Well, I hope the rest of our horses can keep up with him."

"We'll make sure we wait up for you," Clint said. "After all, it's your party."

On the way out, Clint stopped at the bar to tell Rick Hartman what his decision was.

"I'll be leaving in the morning with Hammer and his crew."

"Going down to Mexico, huh?" Rick said. "What a surprise."

"What does that mean?"

"It means I knew you were going even before you did, my friend," Rick said.

"You know me pretty well, huh?"

"Better than you know yourself," Rick said. He put

his hand on Clint's shoulder and said, "Take care of yourself. I know you want to help your friend, but take a real good look at the situation before you rush in."

"Rick," Clint said, "your concern touches me deeply." Clint's tone was lighthearted, but he shook his friend's hand warmly before heading for his hotel.

ELEVEN

Before leaving the saloon, Hammer talked with the redhead, Olga, and she agreed to come to his room after she finished work.

He stepped outside the saloon and took a deep breath. He considered lighting up another of his slim cigars, but then decided against it. He'd smoked enough of them that day. Instead, he crossed the street, heading for the hotel. Maybe he'd catch some sleep before Olga joined him in bed.

As he approached the front of the hotel three figures stepped from the dark and faced him in a semicircle. None of them had a gun in his hand.

"Hello, nigger," Seth Williams said. "I owe you for this." Williams indicated the lump on his head.

"Friend," Hammer said, "this is a mistake."

"There was a mistake made tonight," Seth Williams said, "but you made it."

Hammer spread his legs and allowed his right arm to hang loosely at his side.

"Hey," Morris said, "there's no need for that. We was only gonna teach you a lesson."

"Oh, I see," Hammer said. "No guns, eh?"

"If you want to go for your gun," Williams said, "go ahead."

"Seth," Blake said, "we was only gonna give him a beatin', to teach him—"

"Shut up!" Williams said. "Ain't a darkie alive I can't take with a gun."

"Seth," Morris said, "if you're gonna turn this into gunplay, you're on your own."

"That go for you, Blake?" Williams asked.

"I'm afraid so, Seth."

"Then get lost, both of you," Williams said. "I'll take care of this nigger myself."

Now Hammer folded his hands in front of him.

"I'll let you call it, fat boy," Hammer said. "Guns or fists."

"It'd give me a lot of pleasure to horsewhip you, boy," Williams said.

Hammer decided to put a stop to things as soon as possible. He took two quick steps forward. Williams went for his gun but found Hammer's hand already there. Hammer held the man's gun in his holster with his right hand and swung his left into Williams's ample belly. Williams folded over, the air leaving his lungs. As he fell, Hammer held on to the man's gun, sliding it from its holster. He turned and faced the other two.

"Hey, take it easy," Morris said. "We was only gonna help him teach you a lesson."

"Take him to wherever he lives and tell him next time I see him, I'll kill him."

"Sure, sure," Blake said, "we'll make sure he don't bother you."

Hammer ejected all of the shells from the gun, threw them one way, and tossed the gun the other. That done, he walked past the men into the hotel lobby, where he came face to face with Dan Horne.

"What are you still doin' up?" Hammer asked.

"I thought you might need help," Horne said. "Guess I was wrong."

"That's okay, Horne," Hammer said. "Just keep bein' ready to give it."

Carlotta Cortez couldn't sleep. She was worried about her mother, and all of the others who lived in Los Alamos. What if *El Gigante* did not keep his word? What if he and his *bandidos* attacked the town before the deadline?

No, she could not think that way, or she would drive herself crazy.

She heard footsteps out in the hall. She sat up in bed and rubbed her upper arms. It was probably one of the men—Hammer, or Horne or Van Halen. She made a face when she thought of Van Halen. He was the only one of the men—including Clint Adams— she would never want to go to bed with.

Horne was handsome, and nearest her age, but she had a problem with his being shorter than she was. She knew she was being unfair to him, but she couldn't help it.

Hammer was an intriguing man. She had no problem with his being black. He was tall, well-built, and good-looking, but he never showed the slightest interest in her.

As for Clint Adams, he was not as handsome as Horne, and not as well built as Hammer, but there was something about him that made her think that, given a choice, she would pick him.

She very much hoped that he would be leaving with them tomorrow—for more reasons than one.

• • •

Clint went to bed thinking of Carlotta Cortez.
He'd been looking for a reason to leave Labyrinth,
and for a direction to take when he did, and she and
Hammer had ridden in and given him both.

Of course, Mexico was a long way to go to watch
a woman lick beer off her upper lip, but when the
woman was Carlotta, it seemed worth the trip.

Besides, Hammer was his friend and needed his
help, and Clint couldn't remember the last time he
had refused a friend help.

He also couldn't remember the last time that
agreeing to help a friend didn't turn out to be a
hell of a lot of trouble.

TWELVE

El Gigante looked down at the town of Los Alamos. At his side was his second-in-command, Ricardo Ignacio Taibo.

"I do not know why you gave them so much time, *jefe*," Taibo said.

"You do not understand the subtleties of leadership, Taibo," *El Gigante* said. His real name was Fernando Arturo Gonzales, but he was called *El Gigante* because of his size. He stood nearly six feet nine, a massive man constructed of muscle and gristle. Unlike many men his size, he did not rely completely on his size while he was growing up. He developed not only his body but his mind as well.

"The longer they have to wait," Gonzales explained, "the more frightened they will become, and the more willing they will be to pay tribute."

"What of Carlotta Cortez?" Taibo asked. "I do not think it was a wise idea to let her leave."

"Carlotta," Gonzales said, speaking of the woman he desired above all others, "has gone north to seek help. She will probably come back with *gringo* mercenaries."

"*Sí, jefe,* that is that I mean."

"Taibo, Taibo," *Gigante* said, shaking his head, "use your head. When we crush the *gringos* the town will pay their tribute that much more quickly."

"We are spending much time on a rumor, *jefe.* What Los Alamos is truly is a poor village, with nothing to pay tribute with."

"They are not poor, Taibo," *Gigante* said, "but if it turns out that they are, we will simply destroy the entire town as an example to others."

"And what of Carlotta Cortez?"

"She will come away with us," Gonzales said, "whether she wants to or not."

Taibo had a brief thought of Carlotta Cortez being given to the men for their pleasures, but then thrust the thought from his mind. If *El Gigante* even suspected he was thinking such a thing Taibo might become like a twig in his massive hands—a twig to be broken and discarded.

Taibo sneaked a look at *El Gigante*'s huge hands and shivered.

"Yes, *jefe,*" Taibo said.

El Gigante was having his own thoughts of Carlotta Cortez. As with most men, Fernando Gonzales fell in love with Carlotta at first sight. Unlike most men, he had been trying to use force to make her love him. She had already told him to his face that she could never love a ruthless *bandido.* He, in turn, told her that he would not always be a *bandido.* Soon, when he had enough money, he would become a revolutionary, a hero to the people.

If Carlotta Cortez had not spit at the ground at that very moment, things might have been different. Right then and there *El Gigante* vowed to force her to be his, even if it meant destroying the town that was her home, and everyone in it.

Clint was astride Duke, waiting when Hammer, Horne, Van Halen, and Carlotta came out of the hotel. Hammer looked up at him and grinned.

"Horne," he said, "why don't you and Van Halen go and get our horses so we don't keep Mr. Adams waiting?"

"Sure," Horne said. "Glad you're coming along, Mr. Adams."

Clint nodded to Horne. Van Halen scowled and followed the smaller man to the livery.

Carlotta walked up to Duke and ran her hand up and down his nose. The big gelding tolerated it from her. Anyone else would have been minus a finger just then.

"I, too, am very glad you are coming."

Clint touched the brim of his hat and said, "I'm at the lady's service."

"My entire village will be in your debt," she said, then looked at Hammer and said, "All of you."

"Lady," Hammer said, lighting his first cigar of the day, "that's why we're doin' it."

THIRTEEN

Carlotta rode point, because she was the only one who knew where they were going.

Clay Van Halen and Dan Horne rode right behind her. They rode side-by-side, but they never seemed to talk to one another.

Hammer and Clint rode drag, and they talked incessantly, catching up since the last time they had seen each other.

Hammer's plan was to ride straight through the day, stopping only to give the horses a blow and some water. They wouldn't camp at all until dark.

"Tell me about those two," Clint said, indicating Horne and Van Halen.

"What's to tell?"

"Tell me what you know," Clint said. "I like to know whose hands my life is in."

Hammer agreed, and took a moment to collect his thoughts.

"I met Van Halen about five years ago," Hammer said. "I was workin' a range war in Kansas, and Van Halen was workin' the other side. We were the only two who seemed to think the whole thing

54

was a nuisance. Everyone else seemed to be enjoyin' it—and enjoyin' it too much. Even the two ranchers seemed to be havin' themselves a grand ol' time.

"Well, one day I was ridin' with a group of men, and we run into Van Halen and a bunch of his men. The shootin' started, and before you knew it, he and I were the only ones left standin'.

"We squared off, like we were gonna go at it, but neither one of us had reloaded."

Hammer stopped at that point, and Clint waited a few beats before speaking.

"So?" he finally said. "What happened?"

"We beat each other to death." When Hammer saw that his joke hadn't gone over very big he said, "Okay, okay. We both decided that the whole thing was a bunch of crap. We mounted up and rode off together."

"Did you stay together?"

"For a while," Hammer said. "A couple of months, anyway. We got into enough scrapes durin' that time for me to know that he would watch my back. That's why when this thing came along he was the first one I thought of. Well, the second one."

"And now what's happened?"

Hammer made a face and said, "I wish I knew. He's not the same man I knew five years ago."

"You haven't run into him since then?"

Hammer shook his head.

"Not a sign."

"What's the big difference?"

"He seems real bitter about somethin', and he always seems to be spoilin' for a fight. As for Carlotta, he's always makin' remarks at her. Ya know, personal remarks. I'm surprised the two of them ain't come to blows yet."

"Maybe he'll straighten out."

"I just hope he pulls his own weight," Hammer said.

"What about Horne?"

"Ah, Horne," Hammer said. "Him I only know by reputation. He's young, headstrong, and good with a gun. That's what I heard. So far I've only seen that he's young, and last night he was ready to back me twice."

"Did you know he was so . . . you know, short?"

"No, but I don't see where that matters, as long as he can perform."

"I feel the same way," Clint said.

They rode a few moments and then Hammer said, "But he *is* short, isn't he?"

"Yep," Clint said, "he sure is."

"You know," Hammer said, "the only two I really know we can count on is you and me."

"Against forty."

"Or more."

"Have you got a plan?"

"Not really," Hammer said. He looked at Clint and smiled with a cigar between his teeth. "I'm still working on it."

"Maybe you wouldn't mind if I worked on it, too."

"Hell, no," Hammer said, grinning again, "I could always use a, ya know, older perspective."

Clint was about to reply when Van Halen rode back on them.

"That kid don't hardly talk at all," Van Halen complained. "What are you two yakkin' about back here?"

"We're devising strategy," Clint said.

"What?"

"We're makin' plans."

"Plans?" Van Halen frowned. "Shouldn't we all be in on that, Hammer?"

"No," Hammer said. "I put this group together. I'll make the plans, and I'll give the orders."

"What about him?" Van Halen demanded. "Why are you talkin' things over with him?"

"He needs an older perspective," Clint said.

"Huh? Well, he sure is gettin' an older somethin' from you."

Van Halen kicked his horse and moved ahead of them again, although not back to where he was, exactly. He was now riding just a little behind Horne.

Clint stared after him and then looked at Hammer.

"How come being called old by him bothers me more than being called old by you?"

Hammer grinned around his cigar and said, "Because you know I do it out of love."

FOURTEEN

They made excellent time and crossed the border before dark. They camped just on the other side. Clint didn't know what kind of protocol the four had set up without him, so he offered to cook.

"Carlotta cooks," Hammer said. "It was her choice. She's very good at it, and you know what my cooking is like."

"I remember."

"Well, Van Halen and Horne aren't much better."

"How's her coffee?"

"You'll like it," Hammer said. "It'll make your hair stand up."

Clint rubbed his hands together at the prospect of coffee strong enough to suit his taste.

She prepared bacon and beans, and the coffee was as advertised.

"We'll set up a watch," Hammer said as they ate supper. "The four of us."

"Why not me?" Carlotta asked.

"You do your share," Clint said. "You cook."

"Right," Hammer said.

"Why bother with setting a watch?" Van Halen asked. "Aren't we still days from Los Alamos?"

58

"We don't know if the bandits saw Carlotta leave, or not," Hammer said. "They might anticipate what she's doing and send someone to watch the border."

"How the hell would they even know where we're gonna cross?" Van Halen asked.

"The Rio Grande is long, but there are certain points that are regularly used as crossings," Clint said. "We used one of them."

"Why didn't we cross somewhere else?"

"We didn't have the time to pioneer a new crossing," Clint said. "You've got to take into account depth, strength of current—"

"Don't explain it to him, Clint," Hammer said. "Van, you'll take the first watch. There are four of us, so we'll each only have to watch for two hours. Horne, you'll go next, then Clint, and then me."

Horne nodded, as did Clint.

"You might as well start now, Van," Hammer said.

"I ain't had my coffee."

"Take it with you."

Carlotta poured a cup and handed it to Van Halen. He took it, picked up his rifle, and walked off muttering to himself.

"I better turn in if I've got the next watch," Horne said. "Good night."

Carlotta cleaned up and made sure there was a full pot of coffee on the fire before she turned in.

Hammer and Clint watched her spread her blanket, lie down, and cover herself with it.

"Disconcerting," Hammer said.

"What?"

"Is that the word?" Hammer asked. "It's . . . disconcerting to have a woman like that in a camp full of men."

"That's the word, all right," Clint said.

"We'd better turn in, too," Hammer said.

"I'm thinking," Clint said, "about what you just said to Van Halen."

"About what?"

"About the bandits seeing that Carlotta had gone," Clint said.

"And?"

"What would you do if you were *El Gigante*?" Clint asked. "Waste your men posting them up and down the Rio Grande?"

"No," Hammer said, thinking, "no . . . I know what you're gettin' at. I'd have someone follow her."

"Right."

They both looked around, as if they could see through the dark whether someone was out there or not.

Out in the dark Augusto Valdez watched them, smiling a smile that revealed his two gold teeth. Under the orders of his leader, *El Gigante,* he had been following Carlotta Cortez ever since she left Los Alamos. He had watched as she met with the black man, Hammer, and then followed her when she and the black man split. He had watched as she met with the small *gringo,* and then as she and the small white one had traveled and met with the big black one and the other *gringo.* After that they had all ridden to Labyrinth, Texas, and met with the fourth *gringo.* Now they were riding to Los Alamos, to do battle with *El Gigante* and his men.

It was to laugh, and Valdez did so, silently. Four men against *El Gigante* alone would be laughable, but for four men to think they could do battle with

El Gigante and all his men—the *gringos* were surely crazy.

Valdez settled down and sipped from the bottle of whiskey he had. He was used to sitting in a cold camp, watching Carlotta Cortez and her *gringo* mercenaries. Nothing warmed a cold camp like a bottle of whiskey.

In the morning he would stop following them. It was obvious that they were now on their way back to Los Alamos. It was time for Valdez to ride on ahead of them and tell *El Gigante* what he knew.

He took another drink, just to celebrate the fact that he was going home.

FIFTEEN

Clint and Hammer kept their assumptions to themselves but decided to do something about them as well. When Horne woke Clint for his watch, Clint walked to the fire to get himself a cup of coffee. He then stood up, stretched, and walked around the camp. The point was to attract the attention of whoever was watching them—if someone was watching them. Even if someone was out there, he might be asleep, especially if he was alone. He certainly wouldn't be able to stay up all night. In fact, if he was asleep that would be even better for Clint and Hammer's plan.

Clint made sure he never looked over at Hammer's bedroll. He just hoped that none of the others would wake and notice that Hammer was gone.

With a cup of coffee in one hand and a rifle in the other, Clint continued to walk around the camp. Just in case their watcher was awake, he was moving around just enough to keep his attention.

Out in the dark, Hammer chose a place to start and then started moving in an ever-widening circle around the camp. If someone was out there watching them, he hoped to find him before morning, and

without alerting him. He and Clint had assumed
even further that, come morning, the watcher might
be a watcher no more. His job was probably to tail
Carlotta and find out who and how many she hired.
Now that he had that information, he would probably head back on his own to relay the numbers to *El
Gigante.* If he managed to do that, Hammer, Clint,
and the others would lose the element of surprise,
and also the opportunity to bluff.

Of course, Hammer's argument that he should be
the one to slip off into the darkness included the fact
that he was black. Clint couldn't very well argue
that point.

Because they had waited for Clint's watch, they
had less than four hours to find whoever was watching them. They both would have been just as satisfied if they found there *was* nobody out there. If that
was the case, it might mean that *El Gigante* wasn't
as smart as they thought he was. It was obvious that
if they did find the watcher they'd have to kill him to
keep him from riding back and warning *El Gigante.*
That was another thing in Hammer's favor. He was
more willing to kill the man on sight than Clint was.

He was *much* more willing to kill the man on sight
than Clint was. Clint had suggested tying the man
up and leaving him behind, but Hammer argued
that there was always a chance that the man could
get free. Killing him was the only sure way to keep
him from being a problem.

At that point, Clint had stopped arguing about
who should go out looking for the man.

Augusto Valdez stared down at the whiskey bottle
in his hand, wondering who had drunk all of the

whiskey. There was only about a finger's width left at the bottom of the bottle, and with a shrug he decided that he had better drink it before someone else did.

In camp Clint looked up at the sky. There were still a couple of hours left, but if Hammer hadn't found anyone by now, maybe there was no one out there to be found.

Clint heard something behind him and turned quickly, rifle at the ready.

It was Carlotta, and she blinked and started as he turned on her.

"I am sorry," she said, her hands held out in front of her at chest level. "I did not mean to startle you."

"What are you doing up?" he asked.

"I could not sleep anymore," she said. "I was going to offer to take Hammer's watch. Where is he? He is not in camp."

"Shhh," he said to her. "Come on, let's get a cup of coffee."

He walked her back to the fire and poured her a cup of coffee.

"Don't look into the fire," he warned her. "It will rob you of your night vision."

"What is going on?" she asked in a low voice. "Where is Hammer?"

"I'll explain . . ." he said, and started talking in low tones as well.

Hammer knew that the man would be keeping a cold camp. A fire would have given him away immediately. He was about to give up his search when he heard something. He stopped short, stood still, and listened.

Damned if he didn't hear a man . . . humming?

SIXTEEN

After Clint explained to Carlotta what he and Hammer had surmised and what they were doing about it, she became angry—at herself.

"I am a fool!" she said bitterly.

"Take it easy," Clint said. "We might be wrong about this. And even if we're right, there was no way you could have known."

"Oh, yes," she said, "I should have known. That is the kind of thing Fernando would do."

He frowned.

"Fernando?"

"*El Gigante.*"

Clint found himself leaning forward.

"Wait a minute," Clint said. "You know *El Gigante?*"

"*Sí,*" she said, shifting uncomfortably, "he is in love with me."

"And you?" Clint asked. "Are you in love with him?"

"No," she said, spitting the word. "I hate him. He is an animal."

It had been Clint's experience that when a woman violently denies loving a man, it usually means the opposite. Suddenly he was concerned that he, Hammer, and the others had gotten themselves involved in some sort of personal argument between this *El Gigante* and Carlotta Cortez.

"Carlotta," Clint said, "this is important. Is this all just something personal between you and *El Gigante*? Because if it is, I don't relish getting shot at, or killed, because of a lovers' spat."

"A spat?" she said, frowning.

"A quarrel between two lovers."

"Fernando and I are not lovers!" she said vehemently. "We have never been lovers. I told you, I hate him. He is an animal, a pig. He is threatening my home and my family. He may have already destroyed them! How could you—"

"All right, all right," he said, "calm down. You'll wake the others. I had to ask. After all, you never told anyone that you knew *El Gigante* personally."

"I did not think it was important."

"Well, it is," Clint said. "Tell me how you met."

"All right . . ." she said.

Hammer could see the man, whose back was to him. He was humming to himself some song unknown to Hammer, probably a Mexican song, and he was rocking back and forth. Hammer could see that his right hand was holding an empty whiskey bottle.

Hammer walked up on the man, who didn't seem to hear him at all. He could have easily slit the man's throat from behind, but he decided to talk to him first.

He took out his gun, moved in close to the man, and pressed the barrel to the back of his head.

"Don't move."

The man stopped humming.

"D-do not shoot, *señor*," the man said, his tone pleading. He had already started to sweat, and Hammer could smell the stink of fear. That was good. Hammer wanted the man to be terrified.

"Then just don't move," Hammer said. He reached around and relieved the man of his gun and tossed it away. He searched him further, found a knife, and tossed it into the bushes with the gun. For good measure, he removed the man's bandolier.

"All right," he said, moving around in front of the man, "now we're gonna have a nice little talk, and as soon as I hear an answer I don't like, you are a dead man. *Comprende?*"

"*Comprendo, señor,*" the man said.

She thought a moment, then said, "He and his *bandidos* rode into town. I think they were simply going to buy some supplies and leave, until they realized that this was the town that was run by women. Then they decided to take what they wanted, and we were powerless to stop them. And then Fernando saw me."

"And that was the first time you met?"

"Yes."

"And he fell in love with you?"

"Yes."

"Well," Clint said, "I can't really blame him for that. You must realize that most men fall in love with you at first sight?"

"*Sí,*" she said. "And did you?"

"Well . . ." he said, "uh . . . maybe not in love, but I certainly was . . . impressed. . . ."

"Impressed?"

"Yes, uh, very . . . you are very beautiful, you know—but we're getting off the subject. What happened after *El Gigante* saw you?"

"He introduced himself to my mother," she said. "His name is Fernando Arturo Gonzales, and he asked for my hand in marriage."

"What did your mother say?"

"She told him she would never allow me to marry a filthy *bandido*."

"And what did he say?"

"He hit her, and knocked her down."

Well, that certainly told Clint something about the man. He had no absolutely respect for a man who would hit a woman.

"What happened then?"

"He came to me and asked me to leave Los Alamos with him."

"And you said no?"

"I spit at his feet!" she said, her face assuming a look of distaste at the memory.

Clint leaned forward even more.

"Did he hit you?"

"No," she said. "I thought he would, but he simply said that I would change my mind. He would see to it."

"And this is all part of what is going on?" Clint said. "He wants the town to pay tribute, and he wants you."

She lowered her head and said, "Yes." It was as if she were ashamed.

"Carlotta, you don't believe that this is all your fault, do you?"

She looked up at him and said, "Maybe if I had

gone with him in the very beginning he would not now be threatening my home and my family."

"Family? Do you have more family than just your mother?"

"They are all my family, Clint."

"I see."

Clint was about to say something else when he suddenly noticed Hammer coming in from the darkness. He carried in one hand a bloody knife, and in the other an empty whiskey bottle.

SEVENTEEN

"The silly sonofabitch was toasting the fact that he was going home," Hammer said, "and he drank the whole bottle. He was actually humming to himself when I found him. In fact, that's how I found him."

Carlotta was pouring him a cup of coffee when Van Halen and Horne came walking up to the fire.

"What the hell is going on?" Horne asked, rubbing his eyes.

"It's still dark, for Chrissake," Van Halen complained, running his hand through his forest of hair.

"It won't be for long," Clint said. "Pour them some coffee, Carlotta. They might as well hear this."

She gave them each a cup of coffee, and then Clint and Hammer explained what they had done and why.

"So you did what? Cut his throat from behind?" Van Halen asked.

"No," Hammer said, "I want to make sure he had been sent by *El Gigante,* so I questioned him first."

"And?" Horne asked.

"He admitted that he'd been following Carlotta ever since she left Los Alamos."

"And she never noticed?" Van Halen asked.

"She had no reason to think that she was being followed," Clint said.

"All she had to do was look over her shoulder one time," Van Halen argued, glaring at her. Carlotta lowered her head momentarily, then lifted it and returned his stare, boldly.

"Leave her alone," Horne said.

"What are you, shorty, her protector?"

"That's enough!" Clint said. "Let's hear what else Hammer has to say."

Van Halen glared at everybody but kept quiet.

"Actually, that's it," Hammer said. "Once he told me he was one of *El Gigante*'s men, I slit his throat."

"Just like that?" Horne asked.

"Is there any other way to do it?" Van Halen asked.

Clint looked at the sky and said, "We can have breakfast, or get an early start."

He looked at Hammer, who said, "I'm for starting now. Horne?"

"Sure. Why not? We're awake."

"Van?"

"I'm hungry."

"Have some beef jerky," Hammer said. "You're outvoted."

"That's no surprise," Van Halen said.

"Stop feeling so persecuted," Hammer said harshly. "Let's get the horses saddled."

"I'll break camp," Clint said.

"I will help," Carlotta said.

As they cleaned the coffee pot and other utensils and extinguished the fire, Clint said to Carlotta, "We didn't finish our talk."

"I thought we did."

"We were working on getting you not to blame yourself for any of this."

"That will take some time."

"Well," he said, "at least you admit to the possibility. That's something."

After breaking camp they decided to look at the man Hammer killed. Clint wanted to see if Carlotta recognized him.

"Cover him with a blanket," Clint said to Hammer, "so she doesn't have to see him . . . that way."

"That way" was with a huge, gaping yaw where his throat used to be. When Clint saw it he thought that Hammer had almost cut the man's head off.

"Why baby her?" Hammer said. "There might be some hard times and ugliness ahead. She might as well start seeing some of it now."

Reluctantly, Clint agreed.

When Carlotta looked at the dead man she covered her mouth with one hand.

"I know," Clint said, "it's ugly."

"No," she said, "it is not that. I have seen this man before."

"Where?"

"I do not know."

"You probably saw him in one of the towns where you stopped," Clint said. "He probably got too close to you a couple of times."

Clint turned around and said, "Anybody else recognize him?"

Horne and Van Halen both took a good, close look at the body.

"Never saw him before," Horne said.

"Jesus," Van Halen said, "what'd you use on him, Hammer? An ax?"

"Just my knife."

"You don't know your own strength," Van Halen said.

"Yes," Hammer said, "I do. I just don't believe in doing things halfway. If I'm gonna kill a man, I make sure I kill him."

"We'd better get moving," Clint said.

Clint went to help Carlotta mount her horse—not that she needed help, but he wanted to check on her.

"Are you all right?" he asked.

"Yes," she said. "Why?"

"Well . . . it wasn't a pretty sight. I didn't want you to see it."

She smiled at him, a dazzling smile that he noticed made her nostrils flare. God, he thought, with that mass of hair, the high cheekbones, and flaring nostrils, she looked like something . . . untamed.

"It is kind of you to want to protect me, Clint," she said, "but I have seen ugliness, even death, before."

"Oh? Where?"

"I guess that is something else I did not tell you," she said. "Every town needs *el jefe,* no?"

"Jefe?" he said. "You mean a sheriff?"

"Sí," she said, "a sheriff."

"What's that got to do with this?" he asked.

"In Los Alamos," she said, "I am the sheriff."

As they all mounted up, Clint moved closer to Hammer.

"Did you know that Carlotta was the sheriff of Los Alamos?"

"I think she told me that, yeah," he said.

"Why didn't you tell me?"

Hammer shrugged.

"I guess I didn't think it was important," Hammer said. "Some woman, huh?"

"I'm beginning to realize that more and more," Clint said. "You know, if this fella doesn't return, they might take it as a bad sign."

"I thought about that," Hammer said. "They could decide to move on the town early. If they do, we could be out some money."

"Money?" Clint said. "What about the children in that town?"

Hammer stared at Clint coldly.

"Clint, let's not make any mistakes about why we're doin' this," he said. "You may think of this as some kind of cause, but I'm lookin' at this as a way to make some money. Okay?"

"Okay," Clint said. "I guess I just forgot about the mercenary side of you."

"Take my advice," Hammer said. "Don't."

"No," Clint said, "no, in the future I think I'll see you just as you are."

Hammer smiled and stuck a cigar between his teeth.

EIGHTEEN

"Enter!" *El Gigante* called.

Taibo entered his leader's tent. Gonzales was naked on his mattress, which had been stolen from a hotel. On the mattress with him was one of the bandit women, a fiery, dark-skinned beauty named Angelina. She was naked, and Taibo could not help but stare at her small but firm breasts. This was as close as he would ever come to a naked Angelina.

"What?" *El Gigante* asked.

"Valdez has not returned."

"So?"

"I think we should move now."

"You do, eh?"

"*Sí.*"

El Gigante sat up on his mattress and stared at Taibo. Angelina got up on her knees behind Gonzales, put her hands on his massive shoulders, and pressed her breasts against him.

"It is lucky for us," *El Gigante* said, "that you are not in charge here."

Taibo stared at his leader, then looked away and said, "Yes."

"We will move when I say so," *El Gigante* said.

"*Sí, jefe.*"

"Send out three men to look for Valdez," *El Gigante* said.

"*Sí, jefe.*"

"If they see the *gringos* and Carlotta, they are to do nothing. Understand?"

"*Comprendo.*"

"Take a count and do nothing. Make sure they understand that she is not to be harmed."

"*Sí,* I will make sure."

"If she is harmed," *El Gigante* said, "I will hold you responsible."

"*Sí, jefe.*"

"Now get out."

Taibo backed out, no longer concerned with seeing Angelina's breasts.

"*Mi jefe,*" Angelina said seductively, rubbing herself against his huge body like a cat, "what does that woman have that your Angelina does not?"

El Gigante turned and palmed Angelina's small breasts, laughing aloud. Angelina did not understand why he was laughing.

NINETEEN

"How far are we from the town?" Clint asked Carlotta.

She was seated across the fire from him. Horne was on watch, Van Halen was seeing to the horses. Hammer was seated to Clint's right.

"A day," she said. "We should be there by tomorrow evening."

"How long does that give us to get prepared?" he asked Hammer.

"According to what Carlotta told me," Hammer said, "we'll have six days."

"Do you have a general store in town?" Clint asked.

"General store?"

"A place that sells tools, clothes, supplies—"

"Oh, yes, we have such a store."

"Do you sell explosives?"

She frowned.

"Dynamite? You know . . . boom?"

"We do not have anything that goes . . . boom."

"I've got boom," Hammer said.

"What?" Clint said.

78

"Dynamite."

"You've got dynamite?"

"Sure."

"Where?"

"In my saddlebags."

Clint stared at his friend.

"Are you mad?"

"At you?" Hammer asked. He stuck a cigar in his mouth and smiled at Clint.

"You've been carrying dynamite around in your saddlebags and you didn't tell anyone?" Clint asked. He kept his voice low so neither Horne nor Van Halen would hear.

"Why worry everybody?" Hammer said. "Besides, dyamite's not that dangerous when you know how to handle it."

"And you do?"

"Sure."

"By carrying it around in your saddlebags? In this heat?"

"Hey," Hammer said, "Don't worry. I've got it wrapped in oilcloth."

"Jesus . . ." Clint said, putting his hand to his forehead.

"Carlotta," Hammer said, "we'll be coming into town from the north end. Where is *El Gigante* camped?"

"South of town."

"Good."

"He'll be watching," Clint said.

"I know," Hammer said.

"If he hasn't sent out scouts."

Hammer looked at Clint and both men nodded.

"I'll take Van Halen," Hammer said, "and we'll

leave first, before first light."

"All right."

"What are you doing?" Carlotta asked.

"We're figuring that *El Gigante* will have scouts out looking for us," Clint said, "that is, looking for you and the men you hired."

"We want to keep *El Gigante* from knowing how many of us there are for as long as possible," Hammer said. "If he's sent out scouts, then we'll have to take care of them. Van Halen and I will go out early tomorrow and do that."

"But if they see you—"

"They won't see us with you," Hammer said. "That way, we could just be two *gringos* riding along to nowhere in particular."

"I understand."

"Clint and Horne will ride with you to town. All you have to do is give me directions so that Van Halen and I can find it when we're finished."

"It is simple . . ." she said, and proceeded to give him directions.

"All right," Hammer said. "I'll take the last watch. Clint, I'll wake you before we leave camp."

"Right."

"I'm gonna turn in," Hammer said. "Tomorrow the fun starts."

As Hammer walked to his bedroll, Carlotta looked at Clint and said, "Fun? Does he truly think that this will be fun?"

"Well . . ." Clint said, scratching his head, "I suppose some men wouldn't do this kind of work unless they enjoyed it."

"And you?" she asked. "Do you also believe that this will be fun?"

"No," Clint said, "I don't do this for a living, and I don't do it for fun."

"Why then?"

"You can ask me that?" he said. "You were the one sitting across from me licking beer foam from your upper lip."

"That is why you came?" she asked incredulously, "because you like the way I lick beer from my upper lip?"

"Well," he said, "when you say it, it sounds silly."

She stared at him for a long moment and then gave him a smile that he felt down to his toes.

"It is not silly," she said. "It is—what is the word? Flattering?"

"Yes," he said, "that's the word."

She nodded.

"It is flattering," she said. "I am going to sleep now."

She stood up and started away from the fire, but stopped and turned to face him.

"Besides," she said, "I do not believe that is your only reason. Good night."

"Good night."

He watched her roll herself up for sleep, then picked up the coffeepot and poured himself another cup.

"Enough there for another cup?" Horne asked.

"Sure."

He poured Horne a cup and handed it to him. The man hunkered down on the other side of the fire. He took a look at Carlotta over his shoulder, then looked at Clint.

"That's an impressive woman," he said.

"That she is."

"I believe she'll be in the thick of things when push comes to shove."

"I imagine so."

"Have you and Hammer worked out a plan?"

"We're still working on it."

"Have you done this before?" Horne asked.

"Done what?"

"Gone up against impossible odds."

Clint thought a moment, then said, "Once or twice."

"And you're still alive," Horne said. "What's been the deciding factor in the past?"

"Luck," Clint said without hesitation. "A lot of luck."

"Here's to luck," Horne said, raising his cup.

TWENTY

The four *bandidos* spotted the two riders coming toward them.

"I do not see the woman," one of them said.

Carlos Mendez squinted and could see that neither of the riders was a woman. Mendez had been put in command of the other three bandits and was proud of that fact.

"What will we do, Carlos?" one of the three men asked.

"We will continue to ride toward them," Mendez said. "We do not want to alarm them."

"And then?" another asked. "We kill them?"

Mendez wondered what *El Gigante* would do.

"No," he said, "first we will find out who they are and where they come from."

"And then?"

Mendez looked at his three charges wisely and then said, "Then we will kill them."

"How many do you make out?" Van Halen asked.

"Four."

"Yeah," Van Halen said, "that's what I make it."

"How do you want to play it?"

"Like you always say, Hammer," Van Halen said,

"straight ahead. First chance we get, we kill them all."

"That's a lot of shooting," Hammer said. "Hopefully, we're far enough away from Los Alamos that *El Gigante* won't hear."

"Maybe they will hear," Van Halen said. "Maybe they'll all come running, and we'll die in a glorious hail of bullets." Van Halen looked at Hammer and said, "Of course, we'll take as many of them with us as we can."

Hammer stared at Van Halen for a few moments, then said "Jesus" and shook his head.

"Los Alamos is just over that hill," Carlotta said. "When we reach the crest of the hill, you will be able to look down on it."

"Yes," Clint said, adding, "and we'll also be visible to *El Gigante* from there."

"You're right about that," Horne said. "The ground on the other side of town is even higher than this."

"I didn't think—" Carlotta said.

"We'll have to go around," Clint said. "How much time does that add to the trip?"

"Not much," she said. "Perhaps an hour."

"All right," Clint said, looking at Horne, "then let's do it."

It was then that they heard the shots, sounding as if they were coming from far off.

"Hammer . . ." Horne said. He looked at Clint and said, "If we can hear them—"

"No," Clint said, "I don't even think they can hear the shots in town."

Horne and Carlotta exchanged a glance, which

Clint caught. He knew what they were thinking, because he was thinking the same thing. What were they going to do if Hammer and Van Halen never showed up?

As Hammer and Van Halen got closer to the bandits, Hammer said, "You got the left, I got the right."

"At least there ain't nobody in the middle this time," Van Halen said.

TWENTY-ONE

Just outside Los Alamos, Clint stopped.

"What now?" Horne asked.

"It may not mean anything now," Clint said, "but if we ride into town now we're going to attract a lot of attention."

"When you put it that way," Horne said, "Carlotta's been gone so long that when *she* rides in she'll attract attention."

"That's okay," Clint said. "I just don't want any attention drawn to our arrival."

"Then let her go in first."

Clint looked at Horne and said, "That's a good suggestion, Dan."

Horne felt oddly pleased with Clint's praise.

"Carlotta?"

"I will ride ahead and warn my people not to react when you ride in," she said.

"We'll wait here for about twenty minutes," Clint said, "and then ride in."

She nodded and said, "See you in twenty minutes."

Taibo ran to *El Gigante*'s tent and called out.

"Come," *El Gigante* said.

Taibo entered. *El Gigante* was sitting at his "com-

mand table," which had been made by running a
piece of wood over two barrels. He was eating.

"What is it?"

"Our lookout has spotted Carlotta Cortez."

"Where?"

"She is riding into town."

"And?"

"She is alone, *el jefe*."

"That means nothing," *El Gigante* said. "Her
mercenaries could ride in later. Keep the lookout
and tell him to be alert. I want to know as soon as
someone else rides into town."

"*Sí, jefe.*"

Taibo left the tent, and *El Gigante* picked up a
whole chicken and bit into it thoughtfully.

"Ready?" Clint said, looking at Horne.

"It's like Hammer said," Horne replied. "Now the
fun starts."

When they rode down the main street of Los
Alamos it looked for all the world like a ghost town.
There was no one on the street, and as far as they
could tell, no one was looking out the windows.

As for Los Alamos' main street, it was also the
town's only street.

"This is what we came here to protect?" Horne
asked, looking around.

"What'd you expect for a hundred dollars?" Clint
asked.

El Gigante had started on his second whole chick-
en when Taibo returned.

"What?" *El Gigante* said.

"Two *gringos* have ridden into town."

The big man put down the chicken, licked his fingers, and then turned to look at Taibo. There was grease all around *El Gigante*'s mouth.

"Two?"

"*Sí, jefe.*"

El Gigante frowned. He had expected Carlotta to come back with twenty men. *Gringos* have a habit of believing that they were at least as good as any two Mexicans. He had been looking forward to teaching them the error of their ways. But two?

"That cannot be," he said. "Tell the lookout to remain alert. Perhaps they believe that by riding in a few at a time we will not be able to count."

"*Sí, jefe.*"

Taibo left, and then something alarming occurred to *El Gigante*.

"Taibo!" *El Gigante* called before Taibo could get away from the tent.

"*Sí?*" Taibo answered, sticking his head back into the tent.

"Who is on lookout?"

"Pablo Sanchez."

El Gigante tried to place the man, but with so many at his command . . .

"Can he count?"

"*Sí, jefe,* he can count to twenty."

"Very well," *El Gigante* said, "but tell him to count carefully. His life may depend on it."

"I will tell him."

"Get out."

Taibo left, and *El Gigante* went back to his second chicken.

TWENTY-TWO

Clint and Dan Horne weren't quite sure where to stop, so when they saw the sheriff's office—with the word *Jefe* out front—they directed their horses that way and dismounted.

As they dismounted, the door opened and Carlotta stepped out. She was wearing a badge on her shirt, as if to dispel any doubts they might have had about her claim to being sheriff of Los Alamos.

"Carlotta," Clint said, "we didn't want to be noticed, but we didn't want the town to look deserted."

"This is the way the town has looked since *El Gigante* came," Carlotta said. "Everyone stays indoors."

"I see," Clint said. "Well, if you'll tell us where the livery is we'll put our horses up."

"I'll take care of that," Horne said.

"Okay," Clint said, handing Duke's reins to Horne. "Just don't try to do anything but unsaddle him and rub him down."

"Is it okay if I feed him?"

"It should be," Clint said. "Just watch your fingers."

"Yes, sir," Horne said with a mock salute. Carlotta

told him where the livery was, and he walked the horses over there.

"Come inside," Carlotta said. "My mother is waiting to meet you."

Clint stepped onto the boardwalk and took a moment to look up and down the street. Most of the buildings were one-floor adobe structures. They all could have used a coat of paint. What buildings were made of wood had long since fallen into disrepair. He turned and followed her into the office.

"Clint Adams," Carlotta said, "may I present my mother, Lily Cortez."

Even if Clint hadn't already known, he would have been sure that this woman was Carlotta's mother. She had the same mass of dark hair, with some streaks of gray. She was as tall as her daughter, as full-breasted, with a slightly more regal bearing. Clint's best guess put her at forty-four, although Mexican women had been known to give birth in their teens. She could have been as young as thirty-eight.

She was beautiful. If possible, she was even lovelier than her daughter, because she was totally mature.

Or maybe Clint was just happy to find a woman as beautiful as Carlotta who was closer to his own age.

"*Señora,*" he said, removing his hat, "it is my pleasure."

"It is my pleasure, *señor,*" Lily said. "I am glad you have come to help us."

"Well," Clint said, "half of us are here."

"I explained to Mother that we were waiting for Hammer and Van Halen."

"As I said," Lily said, "I am happy you have come to help, but I fail to see what four men can do against *El Gigante* and his men."

"That remains to be seen, *señora,* but we are here and we are willing to try."

Lily Cortez gave him a dubious look.

"Mother," Carlotta said, "I think when you meet Hammer you will feel differently. He and Hammer are very good at what they do."

"Carlotta," Lily said, "make our guests comfortable. I must get back to the store." She looked at Clint and said, "Mr. Adams, I hope you and Mr. Hammer will dine with me this evening?"

"Of course, *señora,*" he said. "We would be happy to."

"I will see you then."

Clint watched as Lily walked to the door and exited. She had the same purposeful stride as her daughter—or vice versa.

"I'm impressed," he said, tossing his hat on the desk. "I can see where you get it from."

"Get what?"

"All of it," he said. "Your grace, your beauty, your intelligence—"

"You like my mother?"

"Very much," he said. "I think she's beautiful."

Carlotta frowned. For a moment Clint thought she might be jealous of her own mother, but that couldn't be . . . could it?

"Now all we need is for Hammer to get here," Clint said.

"Was there trouble?"

"We heard shots," Clint said. "Could you hear them here?"

"No."

"Good," Clint said. "That means that *El Gigante* couldn't hear them, either."

"He might be dead, then," Carlotta said.

"Maybe."

"What will you do if he doesn't come?"

Clint stared at her and said, "Let's cross that bridge when we come to it, okay?"

"I do not know what that means."

"It means let's not go looking for trouble before it gets here, okay?" Clint said. "First let's see if he shows up. If he doesn't, then we'll worry about what we're going to do."

"All right." She still looked as if she didn't quite understand what he was talking about, but she decided not to pursue the matter.

He looked around the office. At least the inside of this building had been worked on. Of course, the rifle rack on the wall was empty, and the single jail cell he could see did not have a door, but at least the place was clean. He laughed to himself when he realized he had been thinking that it had a woman's touch.

"Should I make some coffee?" she asked. She looked as if she needed something to do.

He looked over at the potbellied stove and saw the usual coffeepot.

"Sure," he said, "why don't you. They'll probably need some when they get here."

If they get here.

Horne, standing in front of the sheriff's office with a cup of coffee, was the first to see them riding into town. He backed up and banged on the door.

"Clint!"

The door opened and Clint stepped out, followed by Carlotta. They all watched Hammer and Van Horne ride down the street until they stopped right in front of them.

"Any problems?" Clint asked.

Hammer grinned around one of his cigars and said, "Nope."

TWENTY-THREE

El Gigante walked over to where the lookout was looking down at Los Alamos. Taibo was standing next to the lookout, Pablo Sanchez.

"Well?" *El Gigante* asked. "Have any more men arrived?"

"*Sí, jefe,*" Taibo said. "They just rode into town."

"Ah, good," *El Gigante* said, rubbing his hands together. "How many?"

Taibo and Sanchez exchanged a glance, and then Taibo said, "Two."

"What?"

Taibo cleared his throat and said, "Two, *jefe.*"

"Two more men?" *El Gigante* said. "That is all?"

"*Sí, jefe.*"

Both Taibo and Sanchez watched their leader very carefully, knowing his vaunted temper.

They were not unrewarded.

"This is an insult!" *El Gigante* shouted. "Four men against my might? How dare they?"

"There is still time, *jefe,*" Taibo said. "Perhaps more men will come yet."

"You stay here, Taibo," *El Gigante* said. "Do not

move. I want to know as soon as more men arrive."

"*Sí, jefe.*"

"If no more men come," *El Gigante* said, "I want my horse saddled in the morning. I will teach them to insult *El Gigante*."

As their leader stalked away, both men wiped sweat from their brow and turned their attention to the town.

TWENTY-FOUR

Clint and Hammer had dinner in a room behind the general store. They ate with Lily and Carlotta Cortez. Van Halen and Horne ate at a small café down the street. They might have complained, except they were served a meal fit for kings by a bunch of Mexican women—some of whom were very pretty. The women treated them like saviors—which was, of course, what they were. Also, some of the younger women had been without a man for a long time, and now there were four of them in their midst.

"I'll tell you something, kid," Van Halen said. "It may get a little cold tonight, but we ain't gonna have to sleep alone."

Horne didn't much like Van Halen, but he couldn't argue with him there, not given the way the women were sizing them up. They were all shapes and sizes, too, but Horne had his eye on this little one. She had dark hair and small, high breasts, and she stood about five feet one.

For the moment, Horne and Van Halen were content.

Down the street Lily and Carlotta served Clint and Hammer their dinner. There was a beef roast and a lot of vegetables. The women grew the vegetables themselves, and butchered one of their few remaining cows to feed their four saviors.

"Excuse me, *señora*," Hammer said when they were all seated, "but if your daughter is the sheriff, does that make you the mayor?"

She smiled and said, "Actually, it is the other way around, *señor*. I have been mayor of Los Alamos for a long time, and it was I who appointed Carlotta sheriff."

"Your daughter told us that there were *some* men in town. Couldn't one of them have served as sheriff?"

"We have seven men in town, *señor*," she said, "and none of them is more qualified for the job than my daughter."

"You and your daughter speak excellent English, *señora*," Clint said. "How is that?"

"I learned English at a young age, *Señor* Adams," Lily explained. "In fact, Carlotta's father was an American. She is actually only half Mexican, and I taught her English very early, in case she ever wanted to go and live in America."

"I see."

"My daughter tells me that you are both working on a plan to defeat *El Gigante*. I am confused. Which of you is in charge?"

Clint answered before Hammer could.

"This is Hammer's job, *señora*," Clint said, "I'm just trying to help in any way I can."

"It was my intention," Hammer said, "to make Clint my partner. As far as anyone is concerned, *señora*, he is as in charge as I am."

"I see," she said. "And just what are your plans

for the four of you to defeat *El Gigante* and his *bandidos*?"

Clint and Hammer exchanged a glance. They had no hard-and-fast plan yet, but neither of them wanted to admit that. It was obvious that Lily Cortez had no confidence in their ability to defeat the *bandidos*. If they admitted to having no plan, she would never have confidence in them.

"Well," Clint said, after a slight nod from Hammer, "one thing we thought of was the way you kill a snake."

"And how is that, *señor*?"

"You cut off the head," Hammer said, "and the body dies."

"*El Gigante* is the head," she said, "and his men are the body?"

"That's right."

"I am afraid, gentlemen, that you will find *El Gigante* very difficult to kill."

"Everyone dies, *señora*," Hammer said.

"That is true," Lily said. "Unfortunately, we cannot afford to wait for him to die of natural causes."

Clint looked at Carlotta. She had said very little while in the presence of her mother, ever since their arrival. It seemed that she deferred to the older woman without question.

They finished dinner and Lily said to Carlotta, "Carlotta, why don't you show our guests to their rooms? I will clean up here."

"Yes, Mother."

She stood up, and Clint and Hammer followed.

"We will talk in the morning, gentlemen. According to *El Gigante*'s decree, you have five days to come up with a plan to defeat him—if he does not decide to attack us early."

"Do we know whether he is a man of his word?" Clint asked.

Lily fixed Clint with a steady stare and said, "He is a *bandido, señor.*"

"Yes," Clint said, and followed Carlotta out of the room.

She walked them through the closed general store and out onto the street.

"Is there anyplace a man could get a drink?" Hammer asked.

"We have a *cantina,*" Carlotta said. "I will have someone there to tend bar for as long as you and your men are here."

"Thank you."

"I will show you to your rooms."

She walked them down the street to what appeared to be the only two-story structure in town. At one time, the adobe building had been the town hotel.

In the lobby she turned and said, "You may take any room in the place. They are all empty. All of the beds are made up."

At that moment Horne and Van Halen entered the lobby, led by a plump woman in her forties. The woman was giggling, and Van Halen was laughing. When the woman saw Carlotta, she stopped laughing, pulled her shawl tightly around her, and left.

"I will see you tomorrow," Carlotta said.

"Or later," Clint said.

She nodded and left.

"Jesus," Van Halen said, clapping his hands and rubbing them together, "what do you think of this place, huh? Wall-to-wall women, all sizes and shapes, and all hungry for a man." He looked at Horne and said, "Did you see the way they was lookin' at us?"

"Rein it in, Van," Hammer said. "We're not here so that you can work your way through every woman in town."

"I could do it, too," Van Halen said to him. "You know that."

"We're setting watches," Hammer said. "Since this is the highest building in town, we'll use the roof."

"I'll take the first watch," Van Halen said.

"You're volunteering?" Clint asked in disbelief.

"Damn right," Van Halen said. "We all got to do our part, right?"

He clapped his hands together and then bounded up the stairs to find the roof.

"Pick yourself out a room first!" Hammer called out to him.

"We did that before dinner," Horne said. "Our gear is already upstairs. I stowed both your gear in rooms. You can switch if you want."

"Thanks, Horne," Clint said. "The *cantina* is open for us, if you're interested."

"I'll be over there in a while."

Horne started for the stairs, then turned and said, "He wanted the first watch so he'd be free the rest of the night."

Clint and Hammer exchanged a glance that said they should have known.

Left alone, both looked around the lobby, then looked at each other.

"The *cantina*?" Clint said.

Hammer nodded and said, "The *cantina* . . . definitely."

TWENTY-FIVE

When they reached the *cantina* they found a small room with a bar and about half dozen tables. There were not enough chairs to fill all the tables, and some of the tables and chairs had missing or shorter legs. They managed to match two chairs to a table and turn their attention to the bartender.

She certainly was worthy of attention.

She was dark-haired, of medium height, slightly chubby, and full-breasted. She was wearing a shawl around her shoulders, but beneath it her dress had a low neck, and her breasts were very much in evidence.

"Hello," Clint said.

"Buenas noches, señores," she said pleasantly. Clint found himself looking at the smooth flesh of her breasts.

"Can we have two beers, please?"

"Sí, señor," she said, *"dos cervezas."*

Carlotta had apparently made sure they had a bartender who understood English. Clint didn't know if she could speak English, but apparently she was able to understand it.

When she brought Clint the beer he asked, "What's your name?"

"Popito, *señor*."

"Thank you, Popito."

"Por nada," she said, giving him a dazzling smile.

Clint brought the beers back to the table and sat down with Hammer.

Hammer leaned over his beer and said, "Have you seen most of the women here?"

"I don't think we've seen most of the women yet," Clint said, "but I know what you mean. Most of the ones we've seen are very attractive."

"Attractive?" Hammer said. "Look at that one behind the bar. The way she's dressed—you know, Van Halen was right about one thing. He *could* go through the women in this town in one night."

"I guess we can't fault him for wanting to," Clint said.

"Hell," Hammer said, "not counting Carlotta and her mother, I've seen half a dozen women I wouldn't mind spending a week in bed with."

"I know," Clint said. He was *not* discounting Carlotta and her mother, Lily, though. They were the two best-looking women he had seen in town.

"There're supposed to be seven men here," Hammer said. "I wonder where they are."

"You'd think the bartender would be a man, wouldn't you?"

"I think we should face facts here," Hammer said. "The women rule this town with an iron hand."

"I think we can go a step farther than that," Clint said. "Lily Cortez runs the town—and her daughter—with an iron hand."

"Did you believe that?" Hammer said. "I wouldn't

have thought anyone could dominate Carlotta like that."

"Well," Clint said, "to be fair, we don't know what their relationship is like."

"Maybe we'll find out before this is all over," Hammer said.

Carlotta and her mother had already had one argument since Carlotta's return to town. That one occurred when Carlotta told her mother how many men she had hired.

"Four?" Lily had said, incredulously. "Only four men?"

"That was all I could get, Mother," Carlotta said. "Most men walked away when I told them what the job was. Those who did not walk away then, did when I told them what the pay was."

"I am disappointed, daughter," Lily said, shaking her head. "I expected much more from you."

"Mother," Carlotta said, "the men I have found are very good—"

"Four men," Lily said, cutting her daughter off. "What could four men do against *El Gigante*?"

"They will think of something," Carlotta said. "One of them is the American legend the Gunsmith, Clint Adams."

"One man," Lily said, "even a legend, cannot hope to stand up against *El Gigante*."

"Mother, please—"

"You better go to your office and wait for them," Lily said. "I will make sure no one approaches them, as you have asked."

"Mother—"

"Go, Carlotta."

Carlotta, never able to stand up to her mother, had turned and left. She'd gone to her office to wait for Clint's arrival.

Now mother and daughter were involved in another dispute. After leaving Clint and Hammer at the hotel, Carlotta rushed back to the general store to talk to her mother.

"Mother," she said, "you showed those men no respect at all."

Lily had not yet finished cleaning the table, and she continued to do so and answered without looking at her daughter.

"When they show me that they deserve my respect, I will give it to them."

"All right, then," she said. "What about courtesy, Mother? You could have treated them—"

Lily Cortez dropped the dishes she was carrying to the floor, where they shattered, startling her daughter into silence.

"I sent you to get some men who could help us fight off *El Gigante,* and what did you come back with? Four men, four *gringos!* What can *they* do?"

Carlotta stared at her mother, her eyes stinging, her face warm. In the past she had always backed away from her mother in situations like this. This time she was determined not to do so.

"They will do whatever they can, Mother," she said, controlling her own temper. "They know what they will be up against, but they agreed to come, anyway."

"That is another thing," her mother said. "Why did they come when no one else would? What did you promise them?"

"I promised them no more than we agreed on," Carlotta said.

"I do not understand these men," Lily said, shaking her head.

"I have spent time with them, and I do not understand them, either . . . but I do respect them."

"Well, I am sorry," Lily said, "but I do not. They must earn my respect."

"I'm sorry, too, Mother," Carlotta said, "but no one can do that. I know this, because I have been trying for years."

TWENTY-SIX

Clint looked up when Carlotta entered the *cantina*. Hammer turned his head to see what Clint was looking at.

"I want to talk to both of you," Carlotta said, coming up to their table.

"Sit down, Carlotta," Clint said. "Do you want something to drink?"

"No."

"What's bothering you?" Hammer asked.

"My mother."

Clint and Hammer looked at each other. They had just been talking about her mother.

"I want to apologize to you," she went on, "to all of you."

"For what?" Clint asked.

"My mother's behavior," Carlotta said. "You see, she's disappointed in me. She expected me to bring back many more men."

"That's not your fault," Clint said.

Carlotta smiled grimly and said, "You would not be able to convince my mother of that."

"I could try, if you like," Clint offered.

"No, thank you," Carlotta said. "It has taken me years to stand up to my mother the way I did tonight."

"You did?" Clint asked.

"I was defending the four of you," she said, "but I might have been defending myself, too."

"Your mother didn't seem to have that much confidence in us," Hammer said.

"She does not."

"You can't really blame her for that, Carlotta. After all, who would expect four men to go up against forty with any success?"

"Jesus," Hammer said, "it sounds bad when you put it like that."

"See?" Clint said to Carlotta. "If we don't have complete confidence in ourselves, how could we expect your mother to?"

"Hey," Hammer protested, "I didn't say I didn't have confidence."

Clint gave Hammer a look that was designed to quiet him, and it did.

"Don't be too hard on your mother, Carlotta," Clint said.

"Why not?" Carlotta asked. "Why shouldn't I be? She is hard on everyone else. She has been hard on me for many years."

"Sounds to me like you and your mother have a lot to talk about," Clint said.

Again, Carlotta's wide, beautiful mouth gave way to a grim smile.

"It is very difficult to talk to my mother," she said sadly. "I believe she blames me for this whole thing."

"We went through that once already, Carlotta," Clint said. "Remember?"

"I remember."

"There's no way this can be your fault. *El Gigante* is the one at fault, and everyone should realize that."

"I do not want to talk about my mother anymore," Carlotta said. "What do you intend to do tomorrow?"

"Well," Clint said, "what we should do is look the situation over."

"Look our opposition over," Hammer said.

"Maybe we should go up and talk to *El Gigante*," Clint said.

"And maybe what we should do," Hammer said, looking at both of them in turn, "is go up and give the big guy a chance to surrender."

Clint looked at Hammer and nodded.

Carlotta looked at both of them, shook her head, and said, "You are both mad."

TWENTY-SEVEN

When Horne relieved Van Halen on the roof, Van Halen hurried down to his room. Waiting for him there was one of the women who had been serving him dinner. She was in his bed, and she was naked.

"Oh, baby," Van Halen said, hurriedly undressing.

When he took off his pants, the woman's eyes widened.

"Aye, qué grande."

"I guess that's pretty good, huh?" Van Halen said. He stood there proudly while his penis came erect. "Ain't seen one like this in a long time, have you, honey."

The woman couldn't take her eyes off of him. She wasn't the youngest of the women who had been serving him, and she wasn't the prettiest, but there had been something about her, a sluttish quality, that made him pick her.

He got on the bed with her and greedily began to paw her big, pillowy breasts. She, in turn, grabbed his penis with one hand and cupped his testicles with the other. Before long he was on his back and she was eagerly mounting him.

Who needed Carlotta Cortez when there was a whole town of women as eager and man-hungry as this one was?

"Carlotta," Clint said, "I have a question that I hope won't insult you."

"Ask it."

"The women in this town—women like Popito, there behind the bar—how long has it been since they've had, uh . . ."

"Since they have had a man?" Carlotta asked.

"Yes."

"It has been a long time since any of us have . . . had a man," she said. "A long time since a child has been born here."

"What's going to happen now that we're here?" Clint asked.

"What do you mean?"

"I mean . . . now that there are four young men in town, how will the women react?"

"Oh . . ." she said. Then she smiled and said, "Oh, I see . . ." She looked away, smiling an amused smile, and then looked at them again.

"I suppose there will be those who might . . . come to your rooms in the middle of the night," she said. "Would that be so terrible for any of you?"

"Well, no . . ." Clint said, frowning. He was a little puzzled by her reaction. "I thought that you might object to the women . . . becoming involved with the men. . . ."

"Why would I object?" she asked. "If a woman and a man want each other . . . is there anything wrong with that?"

"No," Clint said, "I guess not."

"Not so long as it doesn't interfere with what we're here to do," Hammer added.

"That's right."

"Of course," Carlotta said. "Of course." She stood up and said, "I think I will go to sleep now. Good night, both of you. I will see you in the morning."

"Good night," Clint said.

Carlotta started for the door, then turned and said something to Popito in Spanish.

"I've told her to stay here for as long as you want her," she told them.

"That's fine," Clint said. "We won't be here that much longer."

"Where will you take your breakfast in the morning?" she asked.

Clint looked at Hammer and said, "What's wrong with right here?"

"Fine with me."

"In fact, we can make this our headquarters."

Hammer nodded.

"I'll arrange for breakfast," Carlotta said. "Good night."

After she left, Clint said, "How about one more beer before we turn in?"

"Sure."

Popito brought the beers to the table and lingered just long enough to exchange a meaningful glance with Hammer.

"Are you thinking what I think you're thinking?" Clint asked.

"And why not?" Hammer asked, watching Popito return to the bar. "We've been on the trail a long time, and it wasn't easy traveling with a woman who looks like Carlotta and not having . . . thoughts."

"I know that."

"So . . . why not?"

"I don't know," Clint said. "I guess there's no reason . . ."

Hammer looked at his beer, drank half of it, and left the half-full mug on the table.

"You know . . ." Clint said as Hammer stood up.

"What?"

"I hope we haven't been brought here for some kind of . . . breeding purposes."

"Breeding purposes?"

"You heard what Carlotta said," Clint said. "It's been a long time since a child was born here."

"Clint, boy," Hammer said, "why not just admit that we've been dropped into the middle of a candy store. I've never known you to be shy about having a woman."

"I'm not," Clint said. "Good night, Hammer. I'll wake you for last watch."

"See you in the morning."

He watched Hammer walk to the bar and talk with Popito. At one point Hammer ran his index finger down into Popito's cleavage, and she giggled. Finally she came out from behind the bar, and Hammer put his arm around her.

As they walked out together, Hammer called out, "The key to lock up is behind the bar."

Clint waved, and Hammer and Popito left.

After they left, Clint took a little more time over his beer. When he was finished he carried the mugs around behind the bar and left them there. A moment's search yielded the key to the front door. He doused all the lights, then left, locking the door behind him. When he turned, Carlotta was standing there.

"What are you doing out, Carlotta?" he asked.

"The key," she said, indicating his hand. "We will need it to open in the morning and prepare your breakfast."

"Oh," he said, "right." He handed her the key. As she reached for it, their hands touched. She put her hand in his to take the key, and he closed his hand over hers.

"How did you know I'd have the key?" he asked.

"I didn't," she said.

TWENTY-EIGHT

Taibo very tentatively approached *El Gigante*'s tent. From inside he heard two separate and distinct persons breathing very heavily, moaning, and when a woman cried out, he knew it was Angelina, and he knew that his leader was . . . plowing a field that he himself longed to plow.

Instead of dissuading him from interrupting his leader, this urged him forward.

"*Jefe!*"

The noises from inside stopped.

"Come."

Taibo entered. Fernando Gonazles—*El Gigante*—was seated on the edge of his mattress, his legs stretched straight out in front of him. A massive erection jutted from his crotch. Lying on the mattress behind him was Angelina, who was still in the throes of sexual passion. She was licking her lips, running her hands over her body, and muttering, "ooh, *jefe*," over and over again. The tent was filled with the smell of sex, and Taibo had to push away his jealousy and his desire for the naked girl.

"What is it?"

"There were no other men, *jefe*," Taibo said all in one breath. Suddenly he wished he hadn't interrupted them. He closed his eyes and steeled himself for the explosion to come.

"Very well," *El Gigante* said.

Taibo opened his eyes and stared at his leader. *El Gigante*'s left hand was on Angelina's crotch, and he seemed to be stroking the girl absently. The girl was writhing beneath his touch.

"That is all?" Taibo asked.

El Gigante looked at him.

"Have my horse ready in the morning."

"*Sí, jefe.*"

"You will accompany me."

"*Sí, jefe.*"

"Pick out twenty men to accompany us."

"*Sí, jefe.*"

"And now," *El Gigante* said, closing his hand over the hair of Angelina's crotch, "go away."

"*Sí, jefe.*"

Taibo withdrew and had gone only ten feet from the tent when he heard Angelina cry out. There were other women in the camp available to the *bandidos*, but Taibo found that he only desired Angelina. Perhaps, he thought, when they destroyed the town of Los Alamos, one of the women there would appeal to him. *El Gigante* had already promised his men that they could have any woman they wanted from the town below.

TWENTY-NINE

Carlotta took Clint to a room she said she kept at the far end of town, "to get away" from her mother when she had to.

The room was behind what looked like it used to be some kind of store. The storefront was dusty, with broken shelving all around, but when they entered the back room it was spotless, and Spartanly furnished. In fact, there was only a bed and a chair.

They used the bed.

Clint unbuttoned Carlotta's shirt and peeled it off her. Her breasts were all they promised to be. They were heavy and round, yet firm. The skin was smooth, and her nipples dark brown. As he touched her breasts, her nipples sprang to life, and her breathing began to come rapidly. He would like to have gone slowly, but he realized that she had gone without for a long time. There was something pent up inside of her that was bursting to get out— and it was passion.

When she kissed him, their lips met so hard and firmly that he was sure they would both be bruised after one kiss. Her tongue eagerly sought his, swirl-

116

ing about in his mouth until it found what it was looking for.

Clint broke the kiss so he could run his lips over her neck. She leaned back in his arms and he slid his hands down to the small of her back, holding her bent over backward like that, her back arched. He kissed her neck and then moved on to her breasts. Gently he licked her nipples, and sucked them. She moaned and brought herself back up to a standing position. She was almost as tall as he was. Her breasts were crushed to his chest, and they were almost nose to nose. Her lips sought his again and they kissed, gently at first, almost nibbling each other, and then more insistently.

She pushed away from him and pulled his shirt open, popping two of the buttons off. She ran her fingernails over his chest, and then around to his back, removing his shirt at the same time. She backed up then, sat on the bed, and removed her boots. That done, she stood up, undid her pants, and slid them down her long, smooth legs. As she bent over to remove her pants, her breasts hung down but did not sway. They were too firm for that. Her midnight black hair fell down over her breasts, and she stood and tossed her head so that her hair went back behind her shoulders. She stood up straight and tall, her chest thrust out at him, watching him. It was clear that it was his turn.

He undid his gunbelt and laid it over the back of the chair. He sat on the chair to remove his boots, then stood to take off his pants. Naked, his erection pointed to her.

She came forward, wrapped both hands around

his penis almost reverently, and then used it to lead
him to the bed. She pulled him onto the mattress
with her.

"Please," she whispered in his ear, her hands eager
on his body, "it has been a very long time. I do not
wish to wait."

He didn't make her wait. He positioned himself
over her and slid into her easily. She was so wet
and ready that there was no resistance.

Once he was inside of her he slid his hands beneath
her to cup her firm buttocks. He began moving inside
her slowly. She rubbed her palms over his buttocks,
up to his back, and then began to use her nails. She
brought her knees up, spreading herself even wider,
and then wrapped her legs around his waist. He
began to move faster, and she matched him with her
hips. Her breath was coming in quick, short breaths,
exhaling every time he drove into her. Suddenly she
tensed, and he felt her shudder, and then she was
pounding on his back with her fists and his buttocks
with her heels as she mindlessly gave herself up to
the sensations that were flooding through her for
the first time in a long time.

"You're so young," he said to her later. "How could
it have been so long for you?"

Staring at the ceiling, she said, "I left here when I
was sixteen and came back two years ago. I needed
that much time away from my mother to find myself.
That is something else she holds against me."

"What, that you had to go away?"

"That I spent part of that time in Mexico City.
That I had . . . many men while I was away, while
she was stuck here." She fell silent, then whispered,

"Many men . . ." She turned her head on the pillow to look at him. "Do you think me terrible?"

"No," he said, putting his hand beneath her chin, "I think you're wonderful."

He kissed her gently and she rolled into his arms, pressing her body to his.

"Posito," she whispered.

"Hmmm?"

She smiled, her eyes glistening.

"Slowly this time, *cara mia.*"

Still later he slid from the bed. She grabbed for him but got only air.

"Where are you going?"

"I've got to relieve Horne on the roof of the hotel," he said, pulling his pants on.

"I will come with you." She started to throw the sheet off, but he caught it and put it back on her.

"No, you stay here and get some rest."

"Are you truly going to go and see *El Gigante* tomorrow?"

"Why not?" he asked. "We might as well size each other up."

"That will be dangerous."

"I don't think so," he said, pulling his boots on. "Little generals like this always have egos."

"I do not understand."

"He'll try and scare us to death first."

"And then?"

He laughed and said, "We'll probably try to scare him, too. We'll all puff up our chests and try to look tough, while inside we'll all probably be scared."

"Even *El Gigante?*"

"Yes, even *El Gigante.*"

"And even you?"

"Yes," he said, laughing, "even me."

She frowned.

"I cannot ever imagine either one of you being afraid," she said.

He leaned over her and said, "Everybody's afraid sometime, Carlotta. Everyone has something they are afraid of."

He kissed her on the forehead and straightened up, reaching for his gunbelt.

"Like me with my mother."

He strapped on his gun, then sat down next to her and took her hand.

"Carlotta, you're not afraid of your mother," he said. "You're just intimidated by her."

"I do not know what that means."

"It means that she makes you think that you are less than you are."

She looked at him in total shock. She squeezed his hand excitedly and said, "But . . . that is exactly how she makes me feel."

"Well," he said, touching her cheek, "you know what you are, and nothing she says, or anyone else says, can make you less."

She cupped his face in her hands and kissed him tenderly.

"Thank you."

"For what?"

"No," she said, "say *por nada.*"

"Por nada," he said. He walked to the door and said, "I'll see you in the morning."

"For breakfast," she said.

Neither of them suspected that they'd never have time to have breakfast.

THIRTY

Clint had been asleep only two hours when there was a pounding at his door.

"Come on, Clint!" Hammer called from the hall.

"Yeah, yeah," Clint called, crawling from bed. He opened the door, but Hammer didn't bother coming in.

"Come on, get dressed," Hammer said.

"What's up?"

"We're gettin' company."

"What?"

"*El Gigante* is on his way here. Shouldn't take him more than five minutes."

"Jesus," Clint said, "wake Horne and Van Halen."

"I already did," Hammer said. "I had to drag them from the arms of their new sweethearts." Hammer peered into the room at the bed and asked, "Are you alone?"

"Yes, I'm alone," Clint said. "I'll meet you on the street."

"Right."

"Hey, send Horne to wake Carlotta." He described the building where Carlotta had her room.

"I'll take care of it. Meet you downstairs."

121

• • •

When Clint came out the front door of the hotel, there were a lot of people waiting. Aside from Hammer, Horne, and Van Halen, Carlotta was there, plus Lily and half a dozen other women.

"Get these women off the street," Clint called out. "Carlotta!"

Carlotta began talking to the women in Spanish, shooing them off the street.

She turned to Clint then and said, "I am staying."

"Of course you are."

"I am staying, also," Lily said.

Clint pointed at her and said, "No, you're not. This is what we were hired for. You get off the street."

"But you are allowing Carlotta to stay."

"She's the law here," Clint said.

"I am the mayor."

"They're coming!" Van Halen said.

"You get off the street," Clint said to Lily, "or I'll remove you myself."

She glared at him, then turned and stalked off to her store.

"Let's get to the end of the street," Hammer called. "I don't want them to get into town." They all started running.

As *El Gigante* and his men approached the town, he saw five people standing abreast, spread out just enough to block the street completely.

Four men and Carlotta Cortez.

He raised his hand to halt his men.

Hammer stood in the center, with Clint to his left and Carlotta to his right. To his far left was Horne, and to his far right stood Van Halen.

El Gigante was easy to pick out. He made his horse look like a pony.

When the *bandido* leader stopped his men, they all looked each other over.

"Carlotta . . ." *El Gigante* said.

"Sheriff Cortez," Carlotta said.

"Oh," *El Gigante* said, executing a mock bow while still on horseback, "*perdón*, Sheriff Cortez. Are these your mercenaries?"

"We've been retained to protect this town," Hammer said, "and that is what we intend to do."

El Gigante laughed, and his men behind him laughed with him.

"All four of you?"

"Yes," Hammer said.

"The five of us," Carlotta said.

"The five of you, well," *El Gigante* said. "Perhaps we should consider surrendering."

"You don't have to surrender," Hammer said.

"All you have to do," Clint added, "is go away."

El Gigante stared at Carlotta and said, "I came down here to protest an insult, but I see now that I may have been wrong. Perhaps you men will be worthy opponents. What are your names?"

"Hammer."

"Horne."

"Van Halen."

"Adams."

"This is Clint Adams," Carlotta added. "In America he is known as the Gunsmith."

El Gigante stared at Clint in silence.

"Even here in Mexico we have heard of the famous Gunsmith," the man said. "This is an honor, *señor*."

"You'll pardon me if I don't feel the same way," Clint said.

"You misunderstand," *El Gigante* said. "The honor will be in killing you. When I have done that, all of Mexico will know, and they will fear me."

"You've got to do it first," Hammer said.

"Oh, *señor*," *El Gigante* said, "rest assured that I shall do it—that is, of course, if you still insist on staying. You can still get on your horses and ride back to your own country."

"Oh, don't worry, friend," Hammer said, "we're staying."

"*Bueno*," *El Gigante* said, sounding pleased. "You are brave men. That is good. Because you are so brave, I will not change my deadline. The town still has four days to pay my tribute."

"You are too kind," Hammer said.

"Of course," *El Gigante* said, "if the beautiful Carlotta—uh, I mean, Sheriff Cortez—would consent to join me in my camp—"

"She's rather sleep with a gila monster," Clint said.

El Gigante's face clouded, and he stared hard at Clint.

"I see that you speak for Carlotta now, *Señor* Adams," he said.

"I speak for myself, Fernando Gonzales," Carlotta said.

"And what say you?"

"I would never consider living or sleeping with an animal such as yourself."

"You push me, Carlotta," he said threateningly.

"Hey," Hammer said, "we don't need four days, Mr. *Gigante*. Bring your men on now."

El Gigante looked at Hammer and grinned, as if something amused him very much.

"Brave," he said, "but foolish. No, *señor*, you have four days to think over your fate. Perhaps you will be smart and go back to your own country before the allotted time has passed. If not . . ." He shrugged.

El Gigante turned his horse around. His men parted like the Red Sea to let him pass, then reformed behind him and followed.

Clint, Hammer, and the others remained where they were until the *bandidos* were out of sight. Then they congregated right there on the street.

"So," Hammer said, "you think we scared him?"

THIRTY-ONE

Lily Cortez was incensed.

"How dare you speak to me that way, and on the street of my own town!"

"*Señora* Cortez," Hammer said, "we don't have time for this."

They had gone from the street to the *cantina*, where Carlotta had them served coffee but no breakfast. Clint, Hammer, and Carlotta were seated at one table, while Horne and Van Halen remained standing. Lily seemed to have come there specifically to yell at Clint.

"What?" Lily said to Hammer.

"We really don't have time for your temper tantrum," Hammer said. "We have to discuss our course of action, so if you have nothing to contribute, I would ask you to please leave."

Her face turned red.

"I am paying you—"

"You are?" Clint asked. "I thought the town was paying us."

"I represent the town!"

"Look," Hammer said, standing up and taking her by the elbow, "I said we don't have time for this.

We'll discuss your wounded pride later."

He pushed her out the door and returned to the table.

Carlotta stared at Hammer and said, "No one has ever spoken to my mother that way."

"Then maybe it's about time someone did," he said.

"She could still come back in," Clint said.

They all turned to look at the door, but when Lily did not return, they turned back around to tend to business.

"What'd you fellas think?" Hammer asked Horne and Van Halen.

"Well, he sure lives up to his name," Horne said. "He's a big one."

"Did anyone count how many men he had with him?" Van Halen asked.

"No," Hammer said. "Did you?"

"Twenty."

"Probably only brought half of them with him," Hammer said.

"What if," Clint said thoughtfully, "he wanted us to believe that?"

"What do you mean?"

"I mean, what if he doesn't have very many more men than that?"

"Great," Van Halen said. "That would make it, oh, say, twenty-five against four."

"Five," Carlotta said.

"Excuse me, ma'am," Van Halen said, "but so far all we know about you is that you can cook and you look pretty. That badge on your chest don't mean that you can shoot, or be counted on in a fight."

"I can outshoot you," Carlotta said.

Van Halen started to laugh.

"Maybe she can," Horne said.

"Sure," Van Halen said.

"I can prove it," Carlotta said.

"How?"

"I will shoot against you," she said, "here and now."

"Come on," Van Halen said. "Hammer, do we have time for this?"

"As a matter of fact," Hammer said, "I'd like to see how she handles a gun. I'll feel better about using her, then."

Van Halen looked around and saw that the three men were looking at him expectantly. Carlotta had challenged him, and he would lose face if he did not accept the challenge. What would happen, though, if he lost?

No, that was unthinkable.

"All right," he said, hitching up his gunbelt, "all right. Let's do it."

"What shall we shoot?" she asked.

A crafty look came over his face and Van Halen said, "Shot glasses."

Hammer looked at Carlotta and said, "What do you say, Madame Sheriff?"

"Agreed."

"Horne," Hammer said, but Horne was already behind the bar.

"Way ahead of you," he said, grabbing two shot glasses and setting them up on the bar.

"How do you want to do this?" Hammer asked.

"Draw and fire," Van Halen said.

"Separately, or at the same time?" Hammer asked.

"Hey, she challenged me, right?" Van Halen said. "Let her shoot against me. We'll do it together."

Hammer looked at the lady and said, "Carlotta?"

"Agreed."

"Horne," Hammer said, "space those glasses a bit." To Van Halen and Carlotta he said, "Give each other some space."

They moved apart until there were about five feet separating them. Horne set up the glasses to correspond with their positions.

"All right," Hammer said, "I'll count to three, you draw *on* three. Understood?"

"Sure," Van Halen said.

"Understood," Carlotta said.

Clint noticed that Van Halen was nervously twiddling the fingers of his gun hand. Carlotta, on the other, appeared calm.

"One . . ." Hammer said. Secretly he put his money on Van Halen—if the man had anything left.

"Two . . ." Horne wanted Carlotta to take Van Halen down a peg, but he would have bet money that Van Halen would take her.

"Three!"

Both of them drew and fired, and the shot glasses both shattered.

THIRTY-TWO

"I beat her!" Van Halen said, holstering his gun.

He looked around at them, but no one was saying anything.

"You saw it!" he said. "I beat her, didn't I?"

He looked at Hammer, who said, "If you did, it wasn't by much."

"Horne, you saw it," Van Halen said, desperate now for someone to agree with him.

"I don't know," Horne said, hedging, "it may have been a tie."

He looked at Carlotta, who holstered her gun and said nothing. She had proved her point.

"We'll do it again," Van Halen said.

"If you like," Carlotta said.

"Two glasses this time," he said to Horne. "Put up two glasses each."

Horne went behind the bar to get the glasses.

"This is ridiculous," said Clint, who disapproved of "playing" with guns. As far as he was concerned, any kind of shooting contest qualified as "playing" with guns.

"Then you decide," Van Halen said. "Who won?"

"If you two really want to have a contest," Clint

said, "why not put up seven glasses?"

"Seven?"

"First one to shatter seven glasses wins."

"But . . . we would have to reload," Carlotta said

"No, no reloading."

"What are you saying?" Hammer asked, interested now. "Seven glasses with six shots?"

"Exactly," Clint said.

Hammer looked at Van Halen, who said, "It can't be done."

He looked at Carlotta, who said, "I must agree. It is impossible."

They all looked at Horne, who said, "I'd bet that it can't be done."

"How much?" Hammer asked.

"I'm not betting money," Clint said.

"What then?" Van Halen asked.

"If I can shatter six glasses with seven shots," Clint said, "you'll forget about this nonsense so we can get back to work. Agreed?"

Van Halen thought about it, then said, "All right, agreed."

"Well, I don't agree," Hammer said. "I want to bet. Who's willing?"

"Have you seen him do this before?" Horne asked.

"Are you kidding?" Hammer said. "I've never seen this man draw his gun unless he was gonna use it on someone. I've never seen him do any kind of trick shooting."

"Then why is he doing it now?" Horne asked.

"He's just tryin' to prove a point, here," Hammer said, "but I've got enough confidence in him to bet on him. You takin'?"

Horne rubbed his jaw.   •

"We ain't making that much for this job," Horne said. "I'll bet the hundred you're paying me, even up. Bet a hundred to win two."

"Done," Hammer said. "Van?"

"Same bet," Van Halen said. "It can't be done."

"Carlotta?"

"I do not bet," she said, "and I do not think it can be done, but if I was going to bet, I would bet on Clint."

"You don't have to bet money," Van Halen said, looking her up and down.

"You are almost as bad as *El Gigante*," she said. "Are there not enough hungry women in this town for you?"

"All right, that's enough," Clint said. "Horne, set up seven glasses, side-by-side. Space them so the shattered glass from one won't upset the others. The idea is to do each glass with a bullet."

"Can't be done," Van Halen said as Horne set up the glasses.

"Step away from the bar," Clint instructed, and Horne moved.

"You want me to count?" Hammer asked.

"If you want," Clint said. He removed his modified, double-action Colt, checked the loads, and then slid it back into his holster.

"Ready?" Hammer asked.

They all watched Clint and the glasses, looking back and forth from one to the other.

"Ready."

"One . . ." Hammer said. He didn't know what Clint had in mind, but he couldn't wait to see this one.

"Two . . ." Horne and Van Halen were wondering what they would do with their two hundred dollars.

"Three!"

Clint drew faster than any of them could see and fired five shots. Five glasses shattered, a split second behind each other.

Two glasses remained.

"Whooee!" Van Halen whooped. "Two hundred dollars, Hammer!"

"He still has one shot left," Hammer pointed out.

"One shot . . ." Van Halen said, snorting.

Clint looked at them all, then walked around so he was looking down the bar. From his vantage point, the two glasses looked like one, and he treated them as such. He fired his last bullet. It shattered the first glass, kept going, and shattered the second.

He holstered his gun and looked at all of them. Horne and Van Halen gaped at him, Hammer had a slow grin on his face, and Carlotta looked proud and stunned.

Seven glasses with six shots.

"Can we get back to work, now?" he asked.

THIRTY-THREE

Somewhat sobered by Clint's performance, Horne and Carlotta sat down at the table with Hammer. Van Halen remained standing at the bar, muttering something about being "conned."

Clint ejected the spent shells from his gun, reloaded it, and holstered it again.

"Hammer, what kind of shape is that dynamite in?" Clint asked.

"It'll go boom, if that's what you mean."

"I don't know how, but maybe we can put it to good use."

"We're in plain view of the bandits up on the hill, so we can't set the dynamite in the street," Hammer said.

"We'll have to have someone on the roof with it," Clint said.

"Or . . ." Hammer said thoughtfully.

"Or what?" Clint asked.

Slowly Hammer explained what he was thinking, playing it out as he spoke because he hadn't worked it out fully himself yet. When he was done they all had opinions, and Horne had a question.

"Is that fair?"

"What?" Hammer asked, as if he wasn't sure what he had just heard.

"Well, I mean, he has given us four more days. If we make a move against him now . . . well, it just doesn't sound . . . right."

"Right?" Clint said.

"Fair?" Hammer said.

"How old are you, Horne?" Clint asked.

"Twenty-five."

"You want to make it to twenty-six?"

"Well . . . sure."

"Then don't ever use words like 'right' and 'fair' when you're in a war," Hammer said. "The graveyard is filled with guys who wanted to play by the rules."

"When you're in a situation like this, Horne," Clint said, "the rules go out the window."

"Can we forget about the lesson?" Van Halen said. "He'll learn as we go along. When do we start?"

Clint looked at Hammer.

"Tonight?"

Hammer nodded and said, "Why not?"

"Okay," Clint said, "let's set who does what. . . ."

After the plans had been made, Hammer told everyone to get some rest . . . or whatever.

On his way out, Van Halen stopped by Clint and said, "That was a nice con job. Seven glasses with six shots. I'll remember that."

"Take my advice," Clint said. "Before you use it, practice."

Van Halen nodded and left.

Clint went over and sat with Hammer. Carlotta went to the bar and got them a couple of beers.

"It is not too early, is it?" she asked, setting the mugs down on the table.

"It's never too early," Hammer said. "Thanks."

"I will see you back here tonight," she said. She gave Clint the kind of look she had not given any of the others, at any time, and left. Hammer noticed.

"I guess I don't have to ask where you spent the night," Hammer said.

"It just . . . happened."

"You don't have to explain anything to me," Hammer said. "I knew you'd be the one, anyway."

"I didn't," Clint said. "Let's forget about that and talk about tonight."

"Yeah," Hammer said, "we're sort of wingin' it, aren't we?"

"That we are," Clint said.

"How about that kid?" Hammer said. "Askin' if we were playin' fair."

"He's young," Clint said. "He'll learn."

"Speakin' of learnin'," Hammer said, "where did you learn that trick with seven glasses and six shots?"

"Right here."

"What?" Hammer said. "You mean—"

"Yup," Clint said. "That's the first time I ever did it."

THIRTY-FOUR

Back on their hill, the bandits dismounted, one of them taking *El Gigante*'s horse from him. *El Gigante* motioned for Taibo to accompany him to his tent.

Inside the tent, *El Gigante* sat down in a chair that had been stolen from the home of a wealthy rancher. The chair was padded, covered with red leather and silver studs. It was the only chair that *El Gigante* had ever found that was large enough for him.

"What did you think, Taibo?" *El Gigante* asked.

Taibo was flattered that his leader would ask his opinion.

"Well, *jefe*, I think—"

"Never mind," *El Gigante* said, "I do not care what you think."

Taibo closed his mouth.

"The Gunsmith," *El Gigante* said. "Do you know what it means to have that man here?"

"No, *jefe*."

"I will tell you," the big man said. "After I have killed the legendary Gunsmith, not only will all of Mexico fear me, but all of America as well. No longer

137

will my rule be limited to Mexico."

"*Sí, jefe.*"

El Gigante took a deep breath and rubbed his
huge hands back and forth on the leather arms of
the chair.

"Two days."

"*Jefe?*" Taibo said, not sure he had heard right.

"We will give them two days to think about their
fate, and then we will attack and destroy the town."

"B-but *jefe*, you just told them they had four days,"
Taibo reminded him.

"I know what I said, Taibo," *El Gigante* said, "but
they dared to go out and bring men in to combat me.
They went out of the country and brought in a *gringo*
legend to protect them. I will show them that no one
can protect them from the wrath of *El Gigante*, not
even a legendary *gringo* mercenary."

"*Sí, jefe.*"

"Now," *El Gigante* said, "help me off with my
boots."

Taibo bent and helped his leader get his boots off,
which was not an easy task. At one point he had to
straddle one of *El Gigante*'s giant legs, while his
leader placed a foot on his butt and pushed. Taibo
almost went through the side of the tent.

"Your boots are off, *jefe*," Taibo said, breathing
heavily.

"Now go and get me Angelina," *El Gigante* said.

Angelina, Taibo thought as he left the tent, his
Angelina.

Taibo found Angelina sitting off by herself.

"Angelina," he said, "*El Gigante* wants you in his
tent."

She looked up at Taibo and he was surprised to see tears in her eyes, and something else.

Fear.

"Angelina?" he said. "Is something wrong?"

"*El Gigante*, Taibo," Angelina said. "He hurts me."

"Hurts you?"

She nodded and looked at him with the hurt in her eyes now plain to him.

"But . . . I thought you . . . you liked lying with him."

"He's so big," she said, "and so strong. . . ."

She was wearing a silk robe that *El Gigante* had stolen for her, and insisted that she wear so she would be ready for his pleasure at any time. Now she drew back the robe to show Taibo one perfect thigh— perfect except for some ugly, mottled bruises.

"He did that?"

She nodded, closed her robe, and stood up.

"I must go to him before he becomes angry," she said, and walked off.

As Taibo watched her walk away, he swore to himself that he would do something . . . something to keep Angelina safe . . .

THIRTY-FIVE

Van Halen spent his day in his room with more of the town's women. He had passed the word that any woman hungry for a man need only come to his room to have her hunger satisfied.

Van Halen was lying on his bed when there was a knock on the door.

"Come in."

The door opened and a woman walked in—only she wasn't quite what Van Halen had expected.

"*Señor* Van Halen?"

He sat up in bed and stared at her. He had already been with five women since arriving yesterday, but they had all been in their twenties or thirties. This woman was easily forty-five years old. She was short and plump, and not particularly pretty.

"You are *Señor* Van Halen, are you not?"

"Uh, yeah," he said, "but listen—"

She wasn't listening, though; she was undressing. In seconds she was naked, her dress in a heap at her feet. For the second time in two minutes, Van Halen was surprised.

For one thing, her large breasts were round and firm, despite their size. Her nipples were brown, and they were easily the longest nipples he had ever seen. Her belly was far from flat, but it wasn't fat, as he had thought when she came in. This woman was solid. She had chunky buttocks and muscular thighs, and every inch of her flesh was smooth. He could smell her readiness as her odor filled the room, and despite himself his cock was getting hard.

"All right," he said, "a woman's a woman, I guess. Come on up here on the bed and help me undress."

Not only did she help him undress, she literally tore his clothing from him, and then Clay Van Halen went for the ride of his life.

Dan Horne had spent the night with the little girl who had caught his eye at dinner last night. Her name was Maria, and she was all of eighteen years old. She was small, with tiny, perfectly formed breasts, pink nipples as hard as pebbles, and an ass that fit almost perfectly in his hand.

Maria was waiting for Horne when he returned to his room after the meeting. He undressed and got into bed with her, and told her everything they had planned.

"It sounds very dangerous for you, my Dan," she said, cuddling up to him.

"It's dangerous for all of us, Maria," Horne said. "If we can't take care of this Gi—uh, Gigila—"

"El Gigante," she said, laughing at him behind her tiny fist.

"Yeah, if we can't take care of him, then everyone is gonna pay for it."

"There is something else we can do, my Dan," Maria said.

"What's that?"

"We can leave Los Alamos," she said, "you and I. We can leave together and not have to worry about *El Gigante* and his men."

Horne actually thought about that for a moment, and then shook his head.

"I can't do that, Maria."

"Because of your friends?"

"They're not my friends," he told her, "but I agreed to come here with them and do a job, and I have to see it through."

She ran her hand over his smooth, hairless chest and said, "You are a wonderful man, my Dan."

"And you're the girl I've been waiting for, Maria," he said. "When this is all over, I'll take you away from here with me, if you want to go."

"Oh, yes, Dan," she said, "yes, yes. . . ." She turned into him, her hot mouth demanding as she pressed it to his, her hands insistently roving over his body, finding his hardness and caressing it.

"My Dan," she whispered as he slid his leg over her, mounted her, and pierced her. . . .

Hammer and Clint flipped a coin in the *cantina*, and Clint lost. That meant he had to go up on the hotel roof and keep watch until relieved by one of the others.

As Clint was passing Van Halen's room he expected to hear a woman's cries, as had been the case since yesterday. Instead, he heard what sounded like Van Halen crying out. Smiling, he guessed that Van Halen had finally found a woman who could handle him.

Van Halen almost sounded like he was in pain.

Clint laughed and made his way to the roof.

Hammer was a little bit at a loss as to what to do with himself. His weapons were in working order, and he didn't need to touch the dynamite until later. Of course, there was always Popito, or one of the other women—one of the ones Van Halen hadn't yet gone through.

He stopped walking, looked up, and saw that he was standing in front of the general store that Carlotta's mother owned.

He decided to go inside and see if he couldn't calm her down a bit. After all, she was going to dole out their meager earnings for this job.

THIRTY-SIX

When Hammer entered the general store, it was empty except for Lily Cortez. She was standing behind the counter, and when she looked up at him it was obvious that she was still angry. Her eyes narrowed, her nostrils flared, and the color rose in her face. He noticed something that Clint had already noticed: She was at least as beautiful as her daughter, possibly more.

"Can I help you with something?" she asked him.

"Uh, yes," he said, realizing that he had been staring. "I, uh, wanted to apologize for the way I treated you earlier. I could have been, uh, gentler."

She stared at him and then surprised him.

"No," she said, looking down at the counter instead of at him, "you were right. That was the wrong time to argue about my wounded pride. We hired you, and I should let you do your job."

"Well . . ." he said, not sure what to say next. He walked up to the counter, and she looked up at him again.

"Is there something else?"

"Uh, I was wondering if there were any other strangers in town."

"No," she said. "no other strangers. Just you and your . . . *compadres.*"

"What are you doing here?" he asked.

"I was just looking for something to do with the time. . . ."

"No," he said, "I mean here, in this town. A woman as beautiful as you should not be cooped up here. You should be in a big city, wearing beautiful clothes—"

"Stop," she said, lowering her head again.

He stopped, but stood there staring at her.

"When Carlotta's father left us I had nowhere to go. I came here with some other women who were in the same situation. I have been here ever since."

"Leave, Lily," he said. "Leave."

"I cannot," she said. "There are too many people here depending on me."

"And what about you?" he asked. "Who do you depend on? Or are you one of those people who has to be strong all the time?"

"Not all the time," she said. "Just when I am with other people."

"You're with me now," he said, "and you don't have to be strong."

She looked at him and said, "I don't?"

"No," he said. He lifted his right hand and touched her cheek. She leaned into his touch with her eyes closed, and he became bolder. He ran his fingertips down her cheek to her chin, and then to her throat.

"I need someone," she said, "I can . . . rest with . . . just rest. . . ."

She was wearing a simple dress with a string tied at the top. He pulled one end of the strong to untie it. The dress gaped open at the neck, and he slid his hand inside. Lily still had her eyes closed, and she leaned into his touch even more. He rubbed the palm of his hand over one big breast, feeling the nipple react, tightening, hardening. When he closed his hand over her breast she lifted one of her hands and placed it over his through the dress, moaning softly.

With his other hand he reached for the dress and tugged it down so that her shoulders were bare. Still holding one breast, he leaned over the counter and ran his lips down one side of her neck to her bare shoulders. Her skin was hot to the touch, and when he ran his tongue over her she groaned and tightened her hand on his, closing it even more tightly over her breast. Of all the hungry women in town, he realized that Lily was probably the hungriest of all—hungry for a time when she didn't have to be strong, didn't have to be the leader. . . .

He tugged the dress down so that the upper portions of her breasts showed. He ran his tongue over them, then pulled the dress down to her waist in one swift movement. He palmed both of her pear-shaped breasts and lifted them to his mouth so he could kiss and suck the nipples.

"*Dios* . . ." she said, her voice breathy, softer than he might have thought it could be. "I cannot get close to you."

For a moment he misunderstood, thought that she did not want to get close to him, but then he realized that she was referring to the counter between them.

"Is there somewhere . . ." he said.

"The back," she said, "we can go in the back . . . oh, please . . ."

He came around the counter, lifted her in his arms, and carried her into the back.

In the back room he pulled the dress off of her completely and marveled at how smooth and firm her body was.

"How could you have a daughter Carlotta's age?" he asked, shaking his head.

"I was sixteen when she was born."

That made her thirty-eight, his age. If he allowed himself to think about that he might start to feel old.

He undressed while she watched, and then she held out her arms to him and he moved into them. Moments later, he felt anything but old.

THIRTY-SEVEN

They all met in the *cantina* just before dark.

Clint had asked Carlotta to round up as many women—and men—as they had who could fire a gun.

"We don't necessarily need them to fire it accurately," he said. "We'll need the noise to add to the confusion."

"If they do not have to be accurate," she said, "that makes it easier."

She had come through with a dozen people, nine women and three men, the first men that any of them had seen since they had arrived. As promised, they were in their fifties and sixties. Lily was one of the women, as was eighteen-year-old Maria.

Hammer had told Lily to have her people round up whatever guns they had in town. They had come up with eight rifles and four pistols. Clint checked them all over and found them to be in working order.

"All right," Clint said, "let's review."

Horne went first.

"I take four people with me to the roof of the hotel. I also take four sticks of dynamite."

Hammer next.

"I take three people with me to a low roof across from the hotel. I'll also have four sticks of dynamite."

Van Halen.

"Carlotta and I will split the other people between us, and station them and ourselves on both sides of the street."

"Right," Clint said. "I'm going up to the bandit camp, taking the remaining four sticks of dynamite with me."

"I still think I should go up to the camp," Hammer said.

"We've already gone through this," Clint said. "Let's not start changing assignments, now."

"All right," Hammer said, "let's do it."

Before they went outside, Maria clung to Horne and said, "Do not get killed, my Dan."

"I wish you would stay inside," he said, hugging her.

"I cannot," she said. "I must help."

"Well, for Chrissake, don't do anything foolish. Just stay behind cover and fire your gun. Don't worry about hitting anything."

She nodded, and they both went outside.

Clint said much the same thing to Carlotta.

"Keep your people safe," he said. "Tell them not to worry about hitting anything. We just want them to make noise."

"I will tell them."

She hugged him tightly, and went to take her people into position.

• • •

As they started outside, Hammer noticed that Van Halen was limping.

"What's wrong with you?"

Thinking about the time he'd spent with the chubby, forty-five-year-old Mexican woman—God, she had been insatiable—Van Halen said, "Don't ask."

Hammer didn't ask. He let Van Halen go ahead of him, and grabbed hold of Lily's arm.

"I don't want you out there when the lead starts flying, Lily," he said, taking the rifle from her.

"Hammer, that is not fair—"

"You have children in town," he reminded her. "I want you to see that they are safely out of harm's way."

She caught his eyes and held them, then nodded and said, *"Bueno,* I will see to it."

Lily kissed him then, not caring who saw, and said, "Be careful."

"If we're careful," Hammer said, "this might not work at all."

THIRTY-EIGHT

It was not part of the plan for Clint to get himself captured, but that's what happened.

He made his way up the hill in the darkness to a point where he could observe the *bandidos'* camp. Making a quick head count he decided that their estimates had been low and high. The bandits had twenty-five to forty men—probably more like thirty. He also spotted a wagon that held ammunition. That would be a prime target for at least one stick of dynamite. The sticks were tucked into the back and sides of his pants, inside his shirt.

Once he had the camp in sight he circled it, trying to find a good vantage point. There was one tent erected on the campsite, and he was certain this belonged to *El Gigante* himself. That would be another target for a stick of dynamite. If he could throw one in there he'd succeed in cutting off the snake's head. With their leader dead the bandits might even forget about riding down the hill and into town. Clint would have preferred that outcome. He wasn't so confident about the ambush they had constructed for *El Gigante* and his men.

Clint was trying to decide between the ammuni-

tion wagon and the tent as his first target when
something cold and hard was pressed to the back
of his neck.

"Do not move, *señor*."

Clint froze. A hand reached down and removed his
gun from his holster.

This wasn't going according to plan at all.

Clint was ushered into *El Gigante*'s tent with
three men covering him. *El Gigante* was seated in
a large, leather chair that Clint was sure he had
stolen.

"Ah, *Señor* Adams," the bandit leader said, as if
he was very glad to see him. "Welcome to my camp.
Did you come here to assassinate me?"

"Something like that."

"I am disappointed," *El Gigante* said. "I gave you
and your *compadres* four days, *señor*. This is not fair
play."

"Well, let me go," Clint said, "and we'll wait the
four days."

El Gigante laughed.

"You are very amusing, *señor*. No, I am afraid we
cannot let you go. Frankly, I am rather surprised
that you and your friends would risk sending you
up here. You are the most valuable member of your,
uh, group."

"Don't underestimate the others," Clint said.

"Oh, I have no intention of doing so, but they are
certainly not in your class. No, when I send your
body back to town, tied to a horse, I think that
will convince the rest of your *compadres* to leave
Los Alamos. It will also convince the women in the
town that resisting me is folly." *El Gigante* looked

behind Clint at his men and said, "Kill him and send
him back."

"You're not going to kill me yourself?"

"I *am* killing you, *señor*," *El Gigante* said. "They
are my hands."

Clint was grabbed by the elbow from behind and
swung around to face the bandit who had gotten the
drop on him. His gun was in the bandit's belt. The
man was smoking a fat cigar and grinning at him,
revealing tobacco-stained and rotted teeth.

"Andale," the man said.

"Good-bye, Mr. Gunsmith," *El Gigante* said as
Clint was led from the tent.

Outside the bandit put his hand on Clint's upper
back and shoved. Clint walked, with the man behind
him, who was himself flanked by two other bandits.
They were walking toward the ammunition wagon.
Clint could see that there were kegs of gunpowder
on the wagon.

"Before you kill me," Clint said, "how about a
cigar?"

There was no answer.

Clint turned and pantomimed smoking a cigar.

"A cigar, *por favor*?"

The man frowned, then shrugged and took out a
cigar and handed it to Clint.

"Gracias," Clint said. "Uh, how about a light.
Fumar?" He wasn't sure he was saying it right, so
once again he used his hand, this time to strike an
imaginary match. He knew the man spoke English,
because he had done so when he captured him,
unless all he could say was, "Do not move, *señor*."

The man took out a stick match, thumbnailed it to
life, and held it out to Clint. Clint touched the man's

wrist to steady it and lit the cigar with it. That done,
he closed his hand around the man's wrist tightly.
The man frowned and started to say something in
Spanish. With the other hand Clint took a stick of
dynamite out of his shirt and held the fuse to the
match.

All three men's eyes widened, and the other two
started running. The third man, whose wrist Clint
was holding, started trying to pull free of Clint's
grasp.

Clint held the dynamite in front of the man's face
and said, "Drop your gun or we'll both die."

Apparently it never occurred to the frightened
man to shoot Clint. He dropped his gun immediately.

"Please, *señor* . . ."

Clint released the man's wrist. Before the man
could run, Clint grabbed his gun from the man's
belt.

"Go," he said to the man.

As the man ran, Clint turned and threw the dynamite into the ammunition wagon, then dove for cover.

The ensuing explosion lit up the sky.

From his vantage point on the hotel rooftop Horne
saw the explosion. It seemed to light up the entire
hill.

"Get ready," he told his people.

The initial flash lit up the sky so that everyone
on the ground saw and heard it. Carlotta put one
hand over her mouth, hoping that Clint had not
been anywhere near the explosion. After that there

were several explosions in quick succession, and she turned to talk to her people.

Van Halen heard the explosions and drew his gun. His people followed his example and readied their weapons.

Hammer, on a lower rooftop across from the hotel, figured that Clint had found the bandits' ammunition supply. That was why there were smaller explosions succeeding the larger one.

"Look alive, people!" he shouted so that everyone could hear him. "Company's comin'!"

THIRTY-NINE

When the ammunition wagon blew, half a dozen men were blown off their feet. Only two of them got up again, and that suited Clint just fine.

Five men were sitting around a fire, staring at the blaze that was the ammunition wagon. Clint moved in behind them and tossed a stick of dynamite into the fire. When it blew, it killed two of them.

Clint turned and ran toward *El Gigante*'s tent. Using the cigar in his mouth, he lit the fuse and threw the dynamite into the tent. After that, Clint found a hiding place in the bushes.

Just before the tent blew, *El Gigante* appeared at the tent flap. The blast threw him forward, although he never left his feet.

Clint watched as *El Gigante* righted himself and shouted, "Taibo!"

A man came running up to *El Gigante*.

"Take all the men but five and destroy that town!"

The words were spoken in Spanish, so Clint didn't know exactly what was said, but he was hoping that *El Gigante* was sending most of his men to town.

He settled into his hiding place to watch.

•   •   •

"Where is Angelina?" Taibo asked *El Gigante*.

"She was in the tent," *El Gigante* said. "Never mind her. Destroy that town."

"Are you coming?"

"No," *El Gigante* said, looking around. "I am going to find the legendary Gunsmith and skin him alive."

El Gigante stalked off, and Taibo rushed to the tent. When he looked inside he could see that the back of the tent and one side had been blown out. Angelina was lying on her stomach, and Taibo didn't have to turn her over to see that she was dead. *El Gigante* had saved himself and left her there to die.

Taibo turned away, tears stinging his eyes, and went to collect the men for the attack on the town.

Clint watched as twenty men mounted up and rode out of camp, obviously heading for the town.

El Gigante, gun in hand, and five men remained behind, so while twenty men rode down to the town, Clint had his work cut out for him here.

The bandits who were riding down on the town were carrying torches, so it was no secret that they were on their way. Dan Horne called out to warn everyone, and then lit one of the cigars Hammer had given him. He choked, but knew he'd have to keep puffing on it to keep the tip glowing.

On the other roof Hammer lit up, then lined up the dynamite sticks on the ledge in front of him. He had two rifles leaning against the ledge, loaded and ready to go; his pistol in his holster; and a second pistol tucked into his belt.

He was ready.

• • •

"Adams!" *El Gigante* shouted. "Clint Adams, where are you?"

When Clint didn't answer, *El Gigante* instructed his men to spread out and search the area. The first chance Clint had, he slipped from hiding and ducked into *El Gigante*'s ruined tent. When he saw the body of the woman, he felt great sadness, but he'd had no way of knowing—he hadn't *seen* her in there earlier, when he'd been taken to see the bandit leader.

"I'm sorry," he said to her.

He figured that the tent would be the last place they would search, so he decided he'd stay there and wait for *El Gigante* to return. As he looked around he saw a wooden chest in a corner of the tent. It had been knocked over, and open, by the blast, and Clint could plainly see that inside the chest was something that Hammer would be very happy to see. He could see glints of both silver and gold.

Here was Hammer's treasure.

FORTY

As Hammer and Clint had hoped, the bandits charged into town with supreme confidence and abandon. It never occurred to them that there would be any danger waiting for them. The fact that they had no leader would work against them as well.

As they rode into town, both Hammer and Horne lit fuses on sticks of dynamite into the midst of the bandits. Hammer, Horne, Van Halen, and Carlotta were firing their weapons even before the dynamite went off, knocking men off their horses.

It was the beginning of the end for the leaderless *bandidos.*

Clint heard footsteps approaching the tent. He stood next to the flap and as a man stuck his head inside, he used the butt of his gun to knock him unconscious. He had holstered his gun when a man appeared through one of the rents in the tent. Clint drew quickly before the man had a chance to bring his gun up, and fired twice. The man staggered out of sight and fell.

His position now given away, Clint kept his gun in his hand and waited—and he hadn't long to wait.

"Adams!" *El Gigante* shouted. "Inside the tent!"

"I hear you!"

"You are finished, Adams! I have only to send my men in after you!"

Clint looked around, and his eyes fell on *El Gigante*'s bed. He had to move the girl off the bed, which he did quickly and roughly. He then picked up the mattress and held it in front of him.

"Come ahead, *El Gigante!*" Clint said, taking the last stick of dynamite out. "Send them in, and come yourself if you have any courage!"

Clint heard *El Gigante* shout orders to his men and lit the last stick of dynamite. He dropped it into the center of the tent and wrapped himself in the mattress.

The explosion was deafening, and he felt the concussion even through the mattress. He wasted no time in tossing the mattress aside and drawing his gun. Right at the tent flap were the bodies of two men, lying bloody and dead on the ground. The tent was barely standing at this point, the back and sides blown away, the roof hanging and sagging.

He turned quickly as *El Gigante*'s fifth man came through the rent in the rear of the tent. The man fired, and Clint felt pain in his left shoulder. He fired twice at the man, who staggered and fell to one knee. Amazingly, the man tried to raise his gun again, and Clint fired again. Finally the man fell forward onto his face.

Clint turned quickly again, crying out at the pain this caused his shoulder. As he'd expected, *El Gigante* roared into the tent. Clint pulled the trigger twice, but the gun fired only once. The bullet struck *El Gigante* in the shoulder.

El Gigante grinned at Clint and said, "It will take more than one bullet to kill me, *Señor* Gunsmith."

Clint pulled the trigger again, and once again there was an empty click.

Both could now hear the explosions and gunfire from town.

"Hear that, bandit?" Clint said. "You're finished here."

"If I am finished," *El Gigante* said, "so are you."

El Gigante raised his gun and Clint looked around for something to grab, or someplace to go. There was a flap of torn tent hanging from the ceiling and Clint was going to leap and grab it, hoping to bring the rest of the tent down on them. He didn't think he'd make it, but he tensed for the impact of the bullet and prepared to leap.

He heard a shot suddenly, which did not come from *El Gigante*. The bandit leader had not fired. There was a second shot, and *El Gigante* staggered forward, a look of shock on his face.

Another man stepped into the tent, one of *El Gigante*'s men.

El Gigante turned and said, "You?"

"*Sí*, it is me, Taibo," the man said. He cocked his gun again and said, "This is for Angelina."

He fired again and Clint saw *El Gigante*'s body jerk and then fall. Clint looked at Taibo, wondering what would happen now.

Taibo looked at Clint and said, "He hurt her, *señor,* and left her to die, but you killed her."

"I didn't mean—" Clint started, but he saw there was no point.

Taibo cocked his gun, but before he could fire, Hammer appeared through the ruins of the tent and fired. Taibo staggered, dropped his gun, and fell dead next to the body of the girl.

"You all right?" Hammer asked.

"Yeah," Clint said. "Thanks."

Hammer checked all of the bodies in the tent to make sure they were dead.

"There's your treasure, Hammer," Clint said.

Hammer looked at the chest and said, "It belongs to all of us. We'll split it."

"How did things go in town?"

"Better than we could have hoped. The bandits were so confused they were sitting ducks. Some of those people actually hit what they were shooting at."

Clint nodded, then reloaded his gun. When he'd holstered it he said, "Let's get back to town and settle up. I want to be out of here in the morning."

Hammer grinned and said, "Settling up may take longer than that."

EPILOGUE

Settling up took a few days, as Hammer and Lily had to decide who got what from *El Gigante*'s treasure. Finally it was agreed that the treasure would be split evenly between the mercenaries and the town. Hammer agreed to forgo the fee that was promised them. After that, dealing with their half, Clint and Hammer agreed that Hammer should get half of it and that the other half would be split among Clint, Van Halen, and Horne.

Once they had all agreed, they decided to wait until Clint's shoulder healed; then they would leave together.

Hammer explained to Clint what happened when the *bandidos* hit town.

"With the first sticks of dynamite, the bandits were totally confused, and they had no leader to turn to. We picked them off cleanly."

"No one was hurt?"

"Some slight wounds, but no one hurt as badly as you."

"And everyone's performance?"

Hammer knew that Clint was asking about Van Halen.

"Everyone performed fine," he said. "No problems. I told you from the beginning that this would be a piece of cake."

Clint rubbed his shoulder and said, "Sure."

What remained was for everyone to say good-bye. The last night Hammer spent with Lily, Clint with Carlotta, and Horne with Maria. Van Halen spent it hiding from his forty-five-year-old friend, whose name turned out to be Conchita.

"She has outlived four husbands," Carlotta told Clint.

"Seeing Van Halen's condition," he said, "I can see why."

She turned to face him in bed and said, "Will you ever come back to Mexico?"

"I don't honestly know, Carlotta," he said. "But if I do, I'll make sure to visit Los Alamos."

"Your friend Hammer has made a change in my mother."

"Good," Clint said. "How much of a change?"

"Well . . ." she said, "miracles cannot happen overnight, but I think perhaps we will get along better from now on."

"That's good, Carlotta. I'm happy for you."

"And you have made a change in me."

"I don't think there was ever that much to change."

"Well," she said, running her hand over his stomach in ever-widening circles, "you have made me understand that even a legend is a man."

As her hand slipped beneath the sheet and took hold of him he said, "Oh, I'm definitely a man, all right."

Watch for

MUSTANG MAN

124th novel in the exciting GUNSMITH series
from Jove

Coming in April!

RICHARD MATHESON

Author of DUEL

is back with his most
exciting Western yet!

JOURNAL OF THE GUN YEARS

Clay Halser is the fastest gun west of the Mississippi, and
he's captured the fancy of newspapermen and pulp writers
back East. That's good news for Halser, but bad news for
the endless army of young tinhorns who ride into town to
challenge him and die by his gun. As Halser's body count
grows, so does his legend. Worse, he's starting to believe
his own publicity—which could ultimately prove deadly!

*Turn the page
for an exciting chapter from*

JOURNAL OF THE GUN YEARS

by
Richard Matheson

On sale now,
wherever Berkley Books are sold!

BOOK ONE
(1864-1867)

It is my unhappy lot to write the closing entry in this journal.

Clay Halser is dead, killed this morning in my presence.

I have known him since we met during the latter days of The War Between The States. I have run across him, on occasion, through ensuing years and am, in fact, partially responsible (albeit involuntarily) for a portion of the legend which has magnified around him.

It is for these reasons (and another more important) that I make this final entry.

I am in Silver Gulch acquiring research matter toward the preparation of a volume on the history of this territory (Colorado), which has recently become the thirty-eighth state of our Union.

I was having breakfast in the dining room of the *Silver Lode Hotel* when a man entered and sat down at a table across the room, his back to the wall. Initially, I failed to recognize him though there was, in his comportment, something familiar.

Several minutes later (to my startlement), I real-

ized that it was none other than Clay Halser.
True, I had not laid eyes on him for many years.
Nonetheless, I was completely taken back by the
change in his appearance.

I was not, at that point, aware of his age, but took
it to be somewhere in the middle thirties. Contrary
to this, he presented the aspect of a man at least a
decade older.

His face was haggard, his complexion (in my
memory, quite ruddy) pale to the point of being
ashen. His eyes, formerly suffused with animation,
now looked burned out, dead. What many horrific
sights those eyes had beheld I could not—and
cannot—begin to estimate. Whatever those sights,
however, no evidence of them had been reflected
in his eyes before; it was as though he'd been
emotionally immune.

He was no longer so. Rather, one could easily
imagine that his eyes were gazing, in that very
moment, at those bloody sights, dredging from the
depths within his mind to which he'd relegated them,
all their awful measure.

From the standpoint of physique, his deterioration
was equally marked. I had always known him as
a man of vigorous health, a condition necessary to
sustain him in the execution of his harrowing duties.
He was not a tall man; I would gauge his height at
five feet ten inches maximum, perhaps an inch or so
less, since his upright carriage and customary dress
of black suit, hat, and boots might have afforded
him the look of standing taller than he did. He had
always been extremely well-presented though, with
a broad chest, narrow waist, and pantherlike grace
of movement; all in all, a picture of vitality.

Now, as he ate his meal across from me, I felt as though, by some bizarre transfiguration, I was gazing at an old man.

He had lost considerable weight and his dark suit (it, too, seemed worn and past its time) hung loosely on his frame. To my further disquiet, I noted a threading of gray through his dark blond hair and saw a tremor in his hands completely foreign to the young man I had known.

I came close to summary departure. To my shame, I nearly chose to leave rather than accost him. Despite the congenial relationship I had enjoyed with him throughout the past decade, I found myself so totally dismayed by the alteration in his looks that I lacked the will to rise and cross the room to him, preferring to consider hasty exit. (I discovered, later, that the reason he had failed to notice me was that his vision, always so acute before, was now inordinately weak.)

At last, however, girding up my will, I stood and moved across the dining room, attempting to fix a smile of pleased surprise on my lips and hoping he would not be too aware of my distress.

"Well, good morning, Clay," I said, as evenly as possible.

I came close to baring my deception at the outset for, as he looked up sharply at me, his expression one of taut alarm, a perceptible "tic" under his right eye, I was hard put not to draw back apprehensively.

Abruptly, then, he smiled (though it was more a ghost of the smile I remembered). *"Frank,"* he said and jumped to his feet. No, that is not an accurate description of his movement. It may well have been his intent to jump up and welcome me with avid handshake. As it happened, his stand was labored, his hand grip lacking in strength. "How *are* you?" he inquired. "It is good to see you."

"I'm fine," I answered.

"Good." He nodded, gesturing toward the table. "Join me."

I hope my momentary hesitation passed his notice. "I'd be happy to," I told him.

"Good," he said again.

We each sat down, he with his back toward the wall again. As we did, I noted how his gaunt frame slumped into the chair, so different from the movement of his earlier days.

He asked me if I'd eaten breakfast.

"Yes." I pointed across the room. "I was finishing when you entered."

"I am glad you came over," he said.

There was a momentary silence. Uncomfortable, I tried to think of something to say.

He helped me out. (I wonder, now, if it was deliberate; if he had, already, taken note of my discomfort.) "Well, old fellow," he asked, "what brings you to this neck of the woods?"

I explained my presence in Silver Gulch and, as I did, being now so close to him, was able to distinguish, in detail, the astounding metamorphosis which time (and experience) had effected.

There seemed to be, indelibly impressed on his still handsome face, a look of unutterable sorrow. His former blitheness had completely vanished and it was oppressive to behold what had occurred to his expression, to see the palsied gestures of his hands as he spoke, perceive the constant shifting of his eyes as though he was anticipating that, at any second, some impending danger might be thrust upon him.

I tried to coerce myself not to observe these things, concentrating on the task of bringing him "up to date" on my activities since last we'd met; no match for his activities, God knows.

"What about you?" I finally asked; I had no more to say about myself. "What are you doing these days?"

"Oh, gambling," he said, his listless tone indicative of his regard for that pursuit.

"No marshaling anymore?" I asked.

He shook his head. "Strictly the circuit," he answered.

"Circuit?" I wasn't really curious but feared the onset of silence and spoke the first word that occurred to me.

"A league of boomtown havens for faro players," he replied. "South Texas up to South Dakota—Idaho to Arizona. There is money to be gotten everywhere. Not that I am good enough to make a raise. And not that it's important if I do, at any rate. I only gamble for something to do."

All the time he spoke, his eyes kept shifting, searching; was it *waiting?*

As silence threatened once again, I quickly spoke. "Well, you have traveled quite a long road since the War," I said. "A long, exciting road." I forced a smile. "*Adventurous,*" I added.

His answering smile was as sadly bitter and exhausted as any I have ever witnessed. "Yes, the writers of the stories have made it all sound very colorful," he said. He leaned back with a heavy sigh, regarding me. "I even thought it so myself at one time. Now I recognize it all for what it was." There was a tightening around his eyes. "Frank, it was drab, and dirty, and there was a lot of blood."

I had no idea how to respond to that and, in spite of my resolve, let silence fall between us once more.

Silence broke in a way that made my flesh go cold. A young man's voice behind me, from some distance in the room. "So that is him," the voice said loudly. "Well, he does not look like much to me."

I'd begun to turn when Clay reached out and gripped my arm.

"Don't bother looking," he instructed me. "It's best to ignore them. I have found the more attention paid, the more difficult they are to shake in the long run."

He smiled but there was little humor in it. "Don't be concerned," he said. "It happens all the time. They spout a while, then go away, and brag that Halser took their guff and never did a thing. It makes them feel important. I don't mind. I've grown accustomed to it."

At which point, the boy—I could now tell, from the timbre of his voice, that he had not attained his majority—spoke again.

"He looks like nothing at all to me to be so all-fired famous a fighter with his guns," he said.

I confess the hostile quaver of his voice unsettled me. Seeing my reaction, Clay smiled and was about to speak when the boy—perhaps seeing the smile and angered by it—added, in a tone resounding enough to be heard in the lobby, "In fact, I believe he looks like a woman-hearted coward, that is what he looks like to me!"

"Don't worry now," Clay reassured me. "He'll blow

himself out of steam presently and crawl away." I felt some sense of relief to see a glimmer of the old sauce in his eyes. "Probably to visit, with uncommon haste, the nearest outhouse."

Still, the boy kept on with stubborn malice. "My name is Billy Howard," he announced. "And I am going to make . . ."

He went abruptly mute as Clay unbuttoned his dark frock coat to reveal a butt-reversed Colt at his left side. It was little wonder. Even I, a friend of Clay's, felt a chill of premonition at the movement. What spasm of dread it must have caused in the boy's heart, I can scarcely imagine.

"Sometimes I have to go this far," Clay told me. "Usually I wait longer but, since you are with me . . ." He let the sentence go unfinished and lifted his cup again.

I wanted to believe the incident was closed but, as we spoke—me asking questions to distract my mind from its foreboding state—I seemed to feel the presence of the boy behind me like some constant wraith.

"How are all your friends?" I asked.

"Dead," Clay answered.

"*All* of them?

He nodded. "Yes. Jim Clements. Ben Pickett. John Harris." I saw a movement in his throat. "Henry Blackstone. All of them."

I had some difficulty breathing. I kept expecting to hear the boy's voice again. "What about your wife?" I asked.

"I have not heard from her in some time," he replied. "We are estranged."

"How old is your daughter now?"

"Three in January," he answered, his look of sadness deepening. I regretted having asked and quickly said, "What about your family in Indiana?"

"I went back to visit them last year," he said. "It was a waste."

I did not want to know, but heard myself inquiring nonetheless, "Why?"

"Oh . . . what I have become," he said. "What journalists have made me. Not you," he amended, believing, I suppose, that he'd insulted me. "My reputation, I mean. It stood like a wall between my family and me. I don't think they saw me. Not *me*. They saw what they believed I am."

The voice of Billy Howard made me start. "Well, why does he just *sit* there?" he said.

Clay ignored him. Or, perhaps, he did not even hear, so deep was he immersed in black thoughts.

"Hickok was right," he said, "I am not a man anymore. I'm a figment of imagination. Do you know, I looked at my reflection in the mirror this morning and did not even know who I was looking at? Who is that staring at me? I wondered. Clay Halser of Pine Grove? Or the *Hero of The Plains*?" he finished with contempt.

"Well?" demanded Billy Howard. "Why *does* he?"

Clay was silent for a passage of seconds and I felt my muscles drawing in, anticipating God knew what.

"I had no answer for my mirror," he went on then. "I have no answers left for anyone. All I know is that I am tired. They have offered me the job of City Marshal here and, although I could use the money, I cannot find it in myself to accept."

Clay Halser stared into my eyes and told me

quietly, "To answer your long-time question: yes, Frank, I have learned what fear is. Though not fear of . . ."

He broke off as the boy spoke again, his tone now venomous. "I think he is afraid of me," said Billy Howard.

Clay drew in a long, deep breath, then slowly shifted his gaze to look across my shoulder. I sat immobile, conscious of an air of tension in the entire room now, everyone waiting with held breath.

"That is what I think," the boy's voice said. "I think Almighty God Halser is afraid of me."

Clay said nothing, looking past me at the boy. I did not dare to turn. I sat there, petrified.

"I think the Almighty God Halser is a yellow skunk!" cried Billy Howard. "I think he is a murderer who shoots men in the back and will not . . . !"

The boy's voice stopped again as Clay stood so abruptly that I felt a painful jolting in my heart. "I'll be right back," he said.

He walked past me and, shuddering, I turned to watch. It had grown so deathly still in the room that, as I did, the legs of my chair squeaked and caused some nearby diners to start.

I saw, now, for the first time, Clay Halser's challenger and was aghast at the callow look of him. He could not have been more than sixteen years of age and might well have been younger, his face speckled with skin blemishes, his dark hair long and shaggy. He was poorly dressed and had an old six-shooter pushed beneath the waistband of his faded trousers.

I wondered vaguely whether I should move, for I was sitting in whatever line of fire the boy might direct. I wondered vaguely if the other diners were wondering the same thing. If they were, their limbs were as frozen as mine.

I heard every word exchanged by the two.

"Now don't you think that we have had enough of this?" Clay said to the boy. "These folks are having their breakfast and I think that we should let them eat their meal in peace."

"Step out into the street then," said the boy.

"Now why should I step out into the street?" Clay asked. I knew it was no question. He was doing what he could to calm the agitated boy—that agitation obvious as the boy replied, "To fight me with your gun."

"You don't want to fight me," Clay informed him. "You would just be killed and no one would be better for it."

"You mean *you* don't want to fight *me*," the youth retorted. Even from where I sat, I could see that his face was almost white; it was clear that he was terror-stricken.

Still, he would not allow himself to back off, though Clay was giving him full opportunity. "*You* don't want to fight *me*," he repeated.

"That is not the case at all," Clay replied. "It is just that I am tired of fighting."

"I *thought* so!" cried the boy with malignant glee.

"Look," Clay told him quietly, "if it will make you feel good, you are free to tell your friends, or anyone you choose, that I backed down from you. You have my permission to do that."

"I don't need your d——d permission," snarled the boy. With a sudden move, he scraped his chair back, rising to feet. Unnervingly, he seemed to be gaining resolution rather than losing it—as though, in some way, he sensed the weakness in Clay, despite the fact that Clay was famous for his prowess with the handgun. "I am sick of listening to you," he declared. "Are you going to step outside with me and pull your gun like a man, or do I shoot you down like a dog?"

"*Go home*, boy," Clay responded—and I felt an icy grip of premonition strike me full force as his voice broke in the middle of a word.

"Pull, you yellow b——d," Billy Howard ordered him.

Several diners close to them lunged up from their tables, scattering for the lobby. Clay stood motionless.

"I said *pull*, you God d——d son of a b——h!" Billy Howard shouted.

"No," was all Clay Halser answered.

"Then *I* will!" cried the boy.

Before his gun was halfway from the waistband of his trousers, Clay's had cleared its holster. Then— with what capricious twist of fate!—his shot misfired and, before he could squeeze off another, the boy's gun had discharged and a bullet struck Clay full in the chest, sending him reeling back to hit a table, then sprawl sideways to the floor.

Through the pall of dark smoke, Billy Howard gaped down at his victim. "I did it," he muttered. "I *did* it." Though chance alone had done it.

Suddenly, his pistol clattered to the floor as his fingers lost their holding power and, with a cry of what he likely thought was victory, he bolted from the room. (Later, I heard, he was killed in a knife fight over a poker game somewhere near Bijou Basin.)

By then, I'd reached Clay, who had rolled onto his back, a dazed expression on his face, his right hand pressed against the blood-pumping wound in the center of his chest. I shouted for someone to get a doctor, and saw some man go dashing toward the lobby. Clay attempted to sit up, but did not have the strength, and slumped back.

Hastily, I knelt beside him and removed my coat to form a pillow underneath his head, then wedged my handkerchief between his fingers and the wound. As I did, he looked at me as though I were a stranger. Finally, he blinked and, to my startlement, began to chuckle. "The one time I di . . ." I could not make out the rest. "What, Clay?" I asked distractedly, wondering if I should try to stop the bleeding in some other way.

He chuckled again. "The one day I did not reload," he repeated with effort. "Ben would laugh at that."

He swallowed, then began to make a choking noise, a trickle of blood issuing from the left-hand corner of his mouth. "Hang on," I said, pressing my hand to his shoulder. "The doctor will be here directly."

He shook his head with several hitching movements. "No sawbones can remove me from *this* tight," he said.

He stared up at the ceiling now, his breath a liquid sound that made me shiver. I did not know what to say, but could only keep directing worried (and increasingly angry) glances toward the lobby. "Where *is* he?" I muttered.

Clay made a ghastly, wheezing noise, then said, "My God." His fingers closed in, clutching at the already blood-soaked handkerchief. "I am going to die." Another strangling breath. "And I am only thirty-one years old."

Instant tears distorted my vision. *Thirty-one?*

Clay murmured something I could not hear. Automatically, I bent over and he repeated, in a labored whisper, "She was such a pretty girl."

"Who?" I asked; could not help but ask.

"Mary Jane," he answered. He could barely speak by then. Straightening up, I saw the grayness of death seeping into his face and knew that there were only moments left to him.

He made a sound which might have been a chuckle had it not emerged in such a hideously bubbling manner. His eyes seemed lit now with some kind of strange amusement. "I could have married her," he managed to say. "I could still be there." He stared into his fading thoughts. "Then I would never have . . ."

At which his stare went lifeless and he expired.

I gazed at him until the doctor came. Then the two of us lifted his body—how *frail* it was—and placed it on a nearby table. The doctor closed Clay's eyes and I crossed Clay's arms on his chest after buttoning his coat across the ugly wound. Now he looked almost at peace, his expression that of a sleeping boy.

Soon people began to enter the dining room. In a short while, everyone in Silver Gulch, it seemed, had heard about Clay's death and come running to view the remains. They shuffled past his impromptu bier in a double line, gazed at him and, ofttimes, murmured some remark about his life and death.

As I stood beside the table, looking at the gray, still features, I wondered what Clay had been about to say before the rancorous voice of Billy Howard had interrupted. He'd said that he had learned what fear is, "though not fear of . . ." What words had he been about to say? Though not fear of other men? Of danger? Of death?

Later on, the undertaker came and took Clay's body after I had guaranteed his payment. That done, I was requested, by the manager of the hotel, to examine Clay's room and see to the disposal of his meager goods. This I did and will return his possessions to his family in Indiana.

With one exception.

In a lower bureau drawer, I found a stack of Record Books bound together with heavy twine. They turned out to be a journal which Clay Halser kept from the latter part of the War to this very morning.

It is my conviction that these books deserve to be published. Not in their entirety, of course; if that were done, I estimate the book would run in excess of a thousand pages. Moreover, there are many entries which, while perhaps of interest to immediate family (who will, of course, receive the Record Books when I have finished partially transcribing them), contribute nothing to the main thrust of his account, which is the unfoldment of his life as a nationally recognized lawman and gunfighter.

Accordingly, I plan to eliminate those sections of the journal which chronicle that variety of events which any man might experience during twelve years' time. After all, as hair-raising as Clay's life was, he could not possibly exist on the razor edge of peril every day of his life. As proof of this, I will incorporate a random sampling of those entries which may be considered, from a "thrilling" standpoint, more mundane.

In this way—concentrating on the sequences of "action"—it is hoped that the general reader, who might otherwise ignore the narrative because of its unwieldy length, will more willingly expose his interest to the life of one whom another journalist has referred to as "The Prince of Pistoleers."

Toward this end, I will, additionally, attempt to make corrections in the spelling, grammar and, especially, punctuation of the journal, leaving, as an indication of this necessity, the opening entry. It goes without saying that subsequent entries need less attention to this aspect since Clay Halser learned, by various means, to read and write with more skill in his later years.

I hope the reader will concur that, while there might well be a certain charm in viewing the entries precisely as Clay Halser wrote them, the difficulty in following his style through virtually an entire book would make the reading far too difficult. It is for this reason that I have tried to simplify his phraseology without—I trust—sacrificing the basic flavor of his language.

Keep in mind, then, that if the chronology of this account is, now and then, sporadic (with occasional truncated entries), it is because I have used, as its main basis, Clay Halser's life as a man of violence. I hope, by doing this, that I will not unbalance the impression of his personality. While trying not to intrude unduly on the texture of the journal, I may occasionally break into it if I believe my observations may enable the reader to better understand the protagonist of what is probably the bloodiest sequence of events to ever take place on the American frontier.

I plan to do all this, not for personal encomiums, but because I hope that I may be the agency by which the public-at-large may come to know Clay Halser's singular story, perhaps to thrill at his exploits, perhaps to moralize but, hopefully, to profit by the reading for, through the page-by-page transition of this man from high-hearted exuberance to hopeless resignation, we may, perhaps, achieve some insight into a sad, albeit fascinating and exciting, phenomenon of our times.

Frank Leslie
April 19, 1876

J.R. ROBERTS
THE
GUNSMITH

___	THE GUNSMITH #111: GRAND CANYON GOLD	0-515-10528-7/$2.95
___	THE GUNSMITH #112: GUNS DON'T ARGUE	0-515-10548-1/$2.95
___	THE GUNSMITH #113: ST. LOUIS SHOWDOWN	0-515-10572-4/$2.95
___	THE GUNSMITH #114: FRONTIER JUSTICE	0-515-10599-6/$2.95
___	THE GUNSMITH #115: GAME OF DEATH	0-515-10615-1/$3.50
___	THE GUNSMITH #116: THE OREGON STRANGLER	0-515-10651-8/$3.50
___	THE GUNSMITH #117: BLOOD BROTHERS	0-515-10671-2/$3.50
___	THE GUNSMITH #118: SCARLET FURY	0-515-10691-7/$3.50
___	THE GUNSMITH #119: ARIZONA AMBUSH	0-515-10710-7/$3.50
___	THE GUNSMITH #120: THE VENGEANCE TRAIL	0-515-10735-2/$3.50
___	THE GUNSMITH #121: THE DEADLY DERRINGER	0-515-10755-7/$3.50
___	THE GUNSMITH #122: THE STAGECOACH KILLERS	0-515-10792-1/$3.50
___	THE GUNSMITH #123: FIVE AGAINST DEATH	0-515-10810-3/$3.50
___	THE GUNSMITH #124: MUSTANG MAN (April 1992)	0-515-10834-0/$3.50
___	THE GUNSMITH #125: THE GODFATHER (May 1992)	0-515-10851-0/$3.50